Methuselah's Gift

Methuselah's Gift

Mary Elizabeth Edgren

ILLUSTRATED BY

KATHRYN PENK KOCH

THOMAS NELSON PUBLISHERS
Nashville • Atlanta • London • Vancouver

Published in Nashville, Tennessee, by Thomas
Nelson, Inc., Publishers, and distributed in Canada
by Word Communications, Ltd., Richmond,
British Columbia, and in the United Kingdom by
Word (UK), Ltd., Milton Keynes, England.

Library of Congress Cataloging-in-Publication Data

Edgren, Mary Elizabeth.
    Methuselah's gift / Mary Elizabeth Edgren : illustrated by Kathryn
Penk Koch.
        p. cm.
    1. Raccoons—Fiction. 2. Grandfathers—Fiction. 3. Family—
Fiction. 4. Death—Fiction. I. Koch, Kathryn Penk. II. Title.
PS3555.D478M48   1994
813'.54—dc20   94-8672
                                                                    CIP

Printed in the United States of America

1 2 3 4 5 6 7 — 00 99 98 97 96 95 94

To Posie
without whom this story
would never
have been written

A Word of Thanks

To my husband Jim, the love of my life and best friend, for believing in me and in the story even when I didn't and for putting in countless hours editing the story and designing the book.

To Nancy Link Powars, editor and publisher of the original hardcover edition, who, with her husband Wayne, graciously accepted the manuscript for publication, and whose own example as grandparents is excelled only by Methuselah himself.

To editors Lonnie Hull DuPont and Sheryl R. Taylor who were instrumental and so helpful in getting the book reprinted.

To Kathryn Penk Koch, illustrator, artist and friend, who, though she had never before met a raccoon, made me believe, when I first saw her drawings, that my story was true.

To our sons Mark and Tim, who, by a strange coincidence, resemble Trasher and Puddly in the story, and who put in many hours on the computer, typing, editing and preparing the original final typescript.

To Elizabeth, our daughter-in-law, who, though she came into our lives well after the story had been started, inspired the cover painting, and made us feel that we had known her all of her life.

To Phillip, Ryan, Heather, Beth and Peggy—little and big friends whose enthusiasm for raccoons and the forest convinced me that I had at least five possible readers.

Mary Elizabeth Edgren

Contents

A NOTE FROM
THE AUTHOR *xi*

1. THE REFUGEES *1*

2. THE REFUGE *5*

3. THE DISCOVERY *11*

4. A NEW HOME *18*

5. EXPLORATIONS *25*

6. THE MEETING *31*

7. A PROMISE
   TO KEEP *38*

8. A CLOSE CALL *41*

9. THE GIFT *47*

10. TEAMWORK *54*

11. FOR YOU *60*

12. MUD PRINTS *67*

13. HELP *73*

14. THANK YOU *81*

15. A MYSTERY *86*

16. AWAY IN
A MANGER *90*

17. AN ENEMY BECOMES
A FRIEND *100*

18. A CELEBRATION *108*

19. CLUES *115*

20. A HERO *124*

21. AN INVITATION *130*

22. THE BOOK *141*

23. THE EXCHANGE *146*

24. THE SICKNESS *152*

25. THE CURE *158*

26. THE SACRIFICE *165*

27. HOPE *173*

A Note from the Author

Never in my wildest dreams could I have imagined the extent of the repercussions that would come from our "chance" encounter with a band of raccoons one night on a family camping trip! It wasn't that I couldn't immediately see their beguiling nature. (In fact, it was at that moment that I decided to use raccoons as my characters in a story I was planning to write for my daughter.) It was just that I was totally unprepared for the far-reaching effects of that meeting. Little did I suspect that through the extensive intelligence network these cunning animals maintain, a ready-made family would walk out of the woods behind our new home in Washington State, moments after we arrived. The word had been passed to them through a unique raccoon communication system originating in Quebec, where we had first met their relatives.

We believed at the time we put out those first doughnuts on our patio that we had a choice. But, having never read the fine print of our deed, we now realize they "came with the house." Eventually we met and supported about twenty of them and our life has not been the same since.

I could write volumes on what this has meant: from the

dispensing of countless bags of marshmallows to heating their hot chocolate on cold nights; from leaving a party early because it was "time," to being awakened at 5:00 A.M. by little trills from a branch too near our bedroom window (I had last fed the three little beggars at 11:30 P.M.); and from entertaining raccoons *inside* our home (books were examined, curtains readjusted, toys played with—requiring us to post a "NO HUNTING" sign on our front door) to receiving the highest compliment a raccoon can ever pay a human—a tug on my clothing and a look toward the door—a clear invitation to *become* a raccoon and come out to play.

It was not surprising when we once again moved across the country to Virginia (though it took three weeks) to be visited by a new band of furry friends who had doubtless "gotten the word" from their Washington State relatives. Once more, I could write volumes on their various character traits. There was the "gentlemanly," almost regal personality of Gideon; the roughneck, and rather rowdy (as evidenced by the many notches on his ears) lifestyle of Jacob; the cultured refinement of Little Debbie's manners; the blunt, "what you see is what you get" (and the sooner the better) approach of Jael. But I won't. I could never express in words what it feels like to hold a velvet paw, to visit with a raccoon on your lap, to be thanked by one, or even to be told "good-bye" forever by one.

But if I can, in even a small way, help you to understand how thoroughly enchanting these little bandits are, one of my purposes in writing the story will have been accomplished. If, after having read it, you agree with a friend who (having read the manuscript) said, "By the time I went to bed, I felt like a raccoon!" then I will have met my highest expectations. And, if my story says anything more to you than "All About Raccoons," my prayers will have been answered.

> Mary Elizabeth Edgren
> Springfield, Virginia
> 1989

A Further Note

In the summer of 1993 we returned to our home in Washington State. As the "word" is being passed from "furry friend" to "furry friend" back across the country, we look forward to visits by "the relatives" in the very near future. And for you, dear reader, my hope and prayer is still that you will be enriched by this story.

> Mary Elizabeth Edgren
> Lakewood, Washington
> 1994

CHAPTER 1

The Refugees

I T HAPPENED on one of those days when nothing could possibly go wrong, in a beautiful Pacific Northwest forest where hardly anything ever does. Of course, something did go wrong, or this story would never have been told. But let me go back to the beginning and tell you how things were.

If you've ever been in an evergreen forest in the summer, you know the kind of day it was—sparkling and crystal clear. The fragrance of sun-baked fir needles filled the air with a sweetness you could almost taste. Giant Douglas firs towered above the forest floor, while down below lay a different world of softer greens—lush ferns sheltering a carpet of velvet moss and tiny mushrooms poking their heads through decayed logs. An occasional shaft of sunlight filtered through the gently swaying branches of the firs and more delicate cedar and hemlock to shine upon clumps of yellow wood violets still glistening with drops of dew.

But most of all, it was quiet. It had been that way for hundreds of years. A hushed stillness, broken only by the songs of birds and the wind rustling through the branches—like whispers in a great cathedral. That was how it was that day—and every day in the forest.

The animals sensed it first. The difference, I mean. You and I wouldn't have noticed it as quickly. Birds that usually sang joyfully now called to one another in alarm. Animals came out of their holes and began to run wildly in all directions. Even insects buzzed around in frenzy. But it was the wind that brought the news that something was dreadfully wrong. It brought a smell that the residents of this forest did not know—the smell of fire. It was a strange, terrifying smell that prompted every living thing to run. And, run they did, knowing somehow that their lives depended on getting away from that smell of death.

Among that band of terrified refugees was a pathetic little creature, covered with so much soot that it was impossible to tell who or what she was. Only the faint gray band outlining her black mask, revealed her identity. She was a little raccoon with eyes full of fear—a fear that spread through her whole body. She ran as if a fire-breathing dragon were chasing her. And, as the fire hissed and roared, devouring everything in its path, I suppose it did seem like a dragon—at least to a frightened little raccoon—a dragon that threatened to lick her up too with its great tongue of fire.

She seemed to be gaining as she ran, getting farther and farther ahead of the flames. Her fear gave way to courage, as she breathed the clearer air. Her alert ears picked up the sound of rushing, tumbling water. And then she saw it—the brook. Beyond it lay safety. Plunging across, with one final effort she flung herself upon a moss-covered rock, and collapsed.

Her lifeless form was just one of many. Others too had crossed the brook to escape the fire, only to perish from injury or exhaustion on the other side. The fire had finished its deadly work. Everything and everyone in its path had been destroyed. There was no funeral and nobody came to mourn. Only blackened stumps stood like gravestones in a cemetery where once a forest had grown.

Our story would have ended here, had not something truly amazing happened. The little raccoon, lying so still just moments before, stirred. She opened her eyes, surveyed the death-like scene, and came to life. No, actually, she *sprang* to life. Her bright eyes darted from one lifeless body to another. She seemed to be looking for someone in particular, but not finding that someone, she scurried about, calling desperately.

(Now, something happened at this point which makes this story different from almost every other story you've ever heard. While it's possible to see and hear animals in the forest, it's not often you can understand their language. But I'm told that once in perhaps a thousand years or so, it is possible to both hear and understand them. Of course, they don't speak in English, or some other human language, it's just that for some unknown reason, you *do* understand. But this only happens if you are in the right place at the right time. *This* was one of those places and times.)

"Grandfather! Grandfather!" she cried. At the sound of her voice, the other lifeless balls of fur came to life. There were five of them—three adult raccoons and two others, slightly larger than the little one who called to them so desperately. Startled, they looked towards her.

"He's gone!" she cried, choking back tears. "I have to find him! I'm going back across the brook to look for him. I have to find him. I *have* to." And before the others could stop her, she was gone.

CHAPTER 2

The Refuge

HER name was Posie because she loved flowers. In fact, it was her custom every day to gather the prettiest flowers she could find and weave them into a lovely wreath for her head. This day had been no different—at least it had started out no differently. But now the lovely wreath was wilted and hung untidily over one ear.

She crossed back over the brook to the fire-blackened forest she had once called home. Nothing looked familiar to her—everything was changed. Desperately she ran, searching frantically and calling out, "Grandfather, Grandfather!"

The others had joined in the search by now, but it was Posie who found her beloved grandfather at last, and he was safe. He had found shelter in a cave-like enclosure, totally protected from the fire. However, a large boulder had rolled in front of the little cave, hiding him almost entirely. Posie would have missed him as she hurried past if she hadn't heard a faint voice answering her call from a small opening beside the boulder—"Here I am, Little Flower." It was Methuselah, her grandfather.

"Grandfather, are you all right?" she asked.

"Yep," he answered weakly.

Posie realized that the tremendous effort of running had greatly tired her grandfather, and she longed to reach down and stroke his fur just to know for sure that he was still alive. Her fears turned to relief as she stammered, "Oh, Grandfather, I thought you were dead!"

"Now, now, Little Flower, The Maker ain't allowed me to live as long as I have without givin' me some common sense for when my strength was all gone. I'm none the worse for wear. Why, I've been havin' myself a right good think while you're all worn to a frazzle!"

"How could you think at a time like this, Grandfather? And what were you thinking about so hard that you couldn't hear me calling you?" Posie squeezed through the small opening as she asked her grandfather these questions, and curled up at his feet just as she had done many times before when she felt a story coming on. "Grandfather," she repeated, "what *were* you thinking about?"

"I s'pose I was thinkin' about the first time we fled."

"But we never had a fire before," she reminded him.

"'Tweren't a fire, really, and 'tweren't really us who fled, either," he told her. "'Twas our ancestors who fled when they had to leave their home in The Garden."

As her grandfather began his strange story, time went backward for Posie. She felt as if something mysterious and secret were being revealed to her alone, and she drank in every word. She was a curious and imaginative little raccoon, and Methuselah could not help smiling as he glanced down at her wide-eyed gaze and little black nose twitching with excitement.

"But why did they flee, and where did they go?" she asked eagerly. "And who told you, Grandfather?"

"One question at a time, Little Flower! You see, one of our distant ancestors passed the story on. Seth was his name, and he was as true and honest as they come. That's why we know the story he told is true."

"What *is* the story he told, Grandfather?" Posie was getting impatient.

"Well, you see, after The Maker went to all the trouble of making the world and filling it with the likes of us, He did something mighty risky. He added two Uprights."

Posie had heard about Uprights before. Though she had never seen one, she had heard how Uprights walked on only two feet all of the time, and they did not have nearly as much fur as raccoons—in fact, only on top of their heads!

Methuselah

Methuselah continued, "In the beginning, things was fine. The Maker asked the Uprights to give names to our ancestors, and we was on right good terms with them at first. Uncle Seth said that our ancestors could understand the Uprights perfectly in them days. Why, the story's told that in them days we didn't have our masks—you see, we didn't need to hide, because that was . . . *before*."

"Before what, Grandfather?"

"*Before* them Uprights turned on their Maker. And *before* He had to make them leave their beautiful home in The Garden and live on their own. And *before* our ancestors had to leave along with them."

"Oh, I see, Grandfather—just like we had to leave our home because of the fire." A tear trickled down Posie's face.

Methuselah reached over and wiped away the tear. "Yep, and that was when them Uprights began to turn on our ancestors. And, of course, then some of our kind turned on them and became bandits. And that's why 'tis we have masks, Little Flower."

At this, Posie broke in with comments and questions. "Well, I think those Uprights deserved to be sent from their home in the beautiful Garden. After all, they turned against The Maker! They shouldn't even be called 'Upright' anymore. But why did the Uprights turn on our kind? And why did our ancestors leave? Did they turn against The Maker too?"

"One question at a time," replied Methuselah. "True, them Uprights deserved to be sent from their home, but The Maker still loved them. And He loved our kind too. But we was made to serve them, and serve them we did. The Maker Himself took hides from some of our brethren to clothe them—just out of pity. That's when it all started—them Uprights tryin' to kill our kind for meat and skins, and some of our kind tryin' to get revenge. And that was goin' against the way The Maker planned for us to act. So you see, some of us turned against Him too. Yep, it was right of The Maker drivin' them out—though I'm told it near broke His heart seein' 'em leave."

"Whose skins did The Maker use to make clothes for the Uprights, Grandfather?" asked Posie.

"It's hard to say. Some say it was lambs—they bein' the

most innocent and dumb of our brethren. Hard to say, though."

"I feel sad for them," said Posie softly. "I'm glad it wasn't raccoons, though. He must have really loved the Uprights to sacrifice some of our brethren just to make clothes for them."

"That He did, Little Flower, and chances are He still does, though they go against Him more and more each day."

"But you don't, Grandfather."

"Nope. From long before the time of Uncle Seth, there's always been some of us who chose to stay true to The Maker and how He made us. I'm one of 'em. I may have a mask on my face, but I'm not wearin' one in my heart."

"I want to be like you, Grandfather," said Posie. "But it's hard to be true to The Maker when all the others are better off than we are. We don't even have a home anymore. Their life seems so easy when all they have to do is steal their food. They seem happy." Posie yawned.

"'Twould appear so, if treasure and pleasure was all that mattered—but 'taint. It's sleepin' good because your mask is gone from your heart—that's what matters. And speakin' of sleep—" Methuselah looked down at Posie. But it was too late. She was already asleep.

CHAPTER 3

The
Discovery

THE LATE afternoon sun shone through the crack in the cave opening, warming Posie and Methuselah as they slept. They were a study in contrasts—one so young and innocent, the other so old and wise. Methuselah's thick, bushy tail had now turned slightly gray. But it was his face that you could never forget—so kind and sensitive and noble. Like a king, Posie had always felt. And he looked that way, even in sleep. It was no wonder that Posie loved him as she did.

"Here they are, here they are! We found them!" Joyful shouts awoke the two from their deep sleep. Posie opened her eyes and saw two familiar faces peering through the crack—Trasher and Puddly, her two big brothers.

"We've been looking for you for an awful long time!" said Trasher with relief. He was the older of the two, and he was wedging his body between the boulder and rock wall, pushing with all his strength. Perhaps it was the sheer force of his strong muscles which made the rock move, but Posie always felt that his strength came in some mysterious way from the yellow scarf he wore tied gallantly around his neck. Ever since he had begun to wear it, Trasher seemed braver and stronger. She was glad for that strength now.

With one final shove, the boulder was moved enough for both to squeeze through.

"Guess what we found!" Puddly blurted out, as soon as he entered the cave. His face fairly exploded with excitement. He was smaller than his brother, yet Posie admired and loved him as much. Never a day went by when Puddly didn't discover something new or include her in one of his exciting adventures. She tried to think now of what it could be that they had found. Perhaps a ball! She remembered when he had found the first one. It had become his dearest treasure. "Another ball!" she was just about to say. But she never got the words out, for at that moment, the rest of the family arrived.

With shouts of, "At last!" and, "Why didn't you answer?" and, "Are you all right, Grandfather?" they crowded around. The scene was one of confusion, until Tidy-Paw brought order to chaos. She was the mother, and her name fit her well. While all the others were covered with soot, she remained spotless and clean.

"Just look at the soot on your paws!" she exclaimed, expressing her most motherly instincts. Posie shrank back from her mother's disapproving glance. "And you might as well throw that wreath away. It's totally wilted."

Tidy-Paw's words brought a howl of laughter from the rest. It wasn't *what* she said that was so funny. In fact, it was quite normal for Tidy-Paw to be concerned with cleanliness. But the laughter came more from relief than humor. After facing fire, near death, and possible separation from each other as they escaped, Tidy-Paw's scolding brought back a sense of normalcy that had been missing during this whole terrifying day. They laughed out of pure joy—they were alive and well and together! At first, Tidy-Paw did not think it was funny, but eventually she smiled and hugged both Posie and Methuselah.

Throughout all this excitement, Puddly did not forget for one instant the news he was trying to tell Posie. Again he began. "Well, guess what we found!"

Seeker

Tidy-Paw scowled. "This is certainly not the time for riddles, Puddly. Can't you see your grandfather has had enough excitement for one day?"

"I was only trying to get Posie to guess what we found," he argued defensively. "She'll be so excited!"

"Oh mercy," sighed Tidy-Paw. "As if anything else had to happen to us today! I had clean forgotten about it! And Aunt Serenity all by herself minding the helpless little thing!"

"Oh, please tell me," urged Posie eagerly. But her question went unanswered, as Seeker interrupted.

"Quickly, Puddly and Trasher, help me make a stretcher for Grandfather. He's much too tired to walk to our camp." Seeker was the largest of them all—a good and dependable father to Posie, Puddly and Trasher. Never did they find it hard to obey him, and they did so now as they quickly constructed a stretcher.

Then in quiet procession, they made their way through the charred ruins of the forest which had been their home. They walked in silence, overcome with a sense of sorrow and loss, and very anxious about their future. Anxiety turned to dread as they approached the brook, the border of their home, for they knew that in crossing it, they would be in enemy territory. But, instead of an enemy, a familiar figure greeted them. Small, and bent-over, she was busily washing something in the stream, humming to herself as she worked. It was Aunt Serenity. She looked frail and old, and yet, at the same time strong and ageless.

Puddly almost dropped his end of the stretcher and just

about upset Methuselah, yelling, "What's for supper, Aunt Serenity?"

"May The Maker preserve us!" she replied. "Why, a body can't do everything with just two paws!"

Tidy-Paw followed Puddly across the brook, arriving on the other side just in time to rescue a freshly washed berry from his grasp. The others followed except for Posie who could not wait to ask her question. Her nose twitched with curiosity.

"Aunt Serenity, where *is* it?"

"Where's what, Dear?" Aunt Serenity seemed so matter-of-fact about it all.

"What you *found!* Puddly told me you found something!"

"Oh, you mean *him.* Well, he's all safe and snug in the hollow log up yonder. Have a peek, but do hush, My Dear."

All eyes followed Posie as she raced to the log Aunt Serenity had described. It was getting dark, and it took a moment for her eyes to focus as she looked in. Her mouth fell open, and for once, she was speechless. A roar of laughter filled the air, until Aunt Serenity gestured frantically to "hush."

"*Now,* do you know what it is?" whispered Puddly as he arrived at her side.

Regaining her speech, she whispered back, "I thought it was a ball and I was right! It is! It has eyes and a tail and it looks like us! But it still looks most like a furry ball!" (And that's how Furry-Ball got his name!)

Posie had so many questions, and she wished she could get them all answered right then. Seeker had other plans, however, for they needed to gather fir needles for their beds and get safely settled for the night. (Now, while it's true that most raccoons are nocturnal, this family was different. In order to avoid their enemies, they chose to sleep at night. Only occasionally did they cross paths with other raccoons.)

After a simple meal of berries, they turned in to bed.

Aunt Serenity

Posie snuggled up to Furry-Ball, covering him with her tail.

A few moments of silence passed. Then Puddly whispered, "I saw him first."

Posie smiled. She too had been found by her family and she had always wished for a brother or sister. Yet she felt sad as she thought about this little raccoon's mother. "What do you think happened to her?" she asked.

"She must have brought him to safety and then went back for her other children," answered Trasher. "But because of the fire, she never made it. And we couldn't leave him there all by himself. He was just too little."

Posie felt happy as she fell asleep that night. After all the troubles of the day it was good to have a warm bed and a new little brother.

It was still dark when they awoke to the sound of voices taunting them. And then they heard above the others the unmistakable voice of their archenemy, Rabid—the leader of the outlaws.

"So, you finally came over to our side, eh?"

Slinky, another of the outlaws chortled, mocking them. Then Needlenose issued a challenge.

"Wanna have some excitement? Why don't you come with us on a chicken raid?"

"Yeah, c'mon and have some *real* fun!" added Rubbish.

Only one of their enemies was silent. It was Waddler. He always remained in the background.

Methuselah, now quite alert, rose to this new challenge. In his most dignified manner, he climbed out fearlessly, hobbled over to his enemies, looked them right in the eye, and said, firmly, but kindly, "We'll not be botherin' you for long, Gentlemen. We'll be a-changin' our address in the mornin'. Please be so kind as to grant us shelter and peace for this one night, and we'll be a-leavin' for our new home tomorrow."

"Oh will you now, Pops? And just where *is* your new address? In them burned out logs you left behind?" Needle-nose sneered.

Maintaining his composure, Methuselah replied, "The Maker will provide us a home. Of that you can be sure."

Raucous laughter followed, and the enemy band ambled off into the forest. After a pause, a little voice whispered from the hollow log, "But Grandfather?"

"Yes, Little Flower . . ."

"Where *will* we live?"

CHAPTER 4

A
New Home

THE SUN had not yet peeked through the tall fir trees, but Tidy-Paw was already down at the stream washing breakfast. Posie, startled to find another furry body next to hers when she awoke, suddenly remembered all the events of the past day. She was deeply grateful to have a new little brother, and she vowed right then to be a good influence on him as well as to protect him. She crept quietly away from the hollow log, careful not to wake Furry-Ball.

"Oh, Mother," she whispered, "He's so cute! Was I that cute when you found me?"

"Yes, dear—only a bit older."

"He already has his mask and five rings on his tail just like us! Was I covered with soft gray fur like Furry-Ball too?"

"Yes," smiled Tidy-Paw. Then staring off into space for a minute, she recalled that special time long ago when Posie arrived.

What a day it had been! Trasher and Puddly had secretly been visiting their friend Waddler and on their way home had been caught in a thunderstorm. Taking shelter under a large fallen tree, they were surprised to find two beady little eyes meeting theirs, accompanied by a pitiful whimper. Trasher and Puddly, though unaccustomed to babies, and a girl at that, felt immediately drawn to this little one. Comforting her, they took turns carrying her home after the rain had stopped. She made herself at home right away, and soon the whole family felt as if she had always been a member. Posie herself could not remember when she had not been in this family. Later, they learned that her mother had been killed by a falling tree.

Her thoughts returning to the present, Tidy-Paw repeated, "Yes, your fur *was* gray just like Furry-Ball's—and just as soft. But he is younger than you were and he'll need lots of help from all of us."

"Oh, I *will* help, Mother. I just love him already. Should I wake him up for breakfast?"

"No, dear—he needs lots of sleep. He'll let us know when he's hungry. But you can help wash these berries."

Posie longed to take another peek at her new little brother, but she obediently helped her mother prepare breakfast.

Soon the others awoke, and rubbing the sleep out of their eyes, made their way to the family circle—all that is, except Methuselah. He was sleeping soundly and no one wanted to wake him. Trasher put their thoughts into words.

"Father, where does Grandfather intend for us to settle?"

"I don't know exactly," replied Seeker.

"This seems like a perfectly good spot here. Why don't we stay? It's certain we won't find food or shelter on the other side of the stream. There's not a tree left from the fire."

"I don't think Grandfather will settle on this side, Trasher. This is enemy territory, remember? Didn't last night's visitors convince you of that?"

"Oh, Father, they're not really so bad—they just seem that way. Waddler's really okay when you get to know him. We could get along, and besides, we need food."

"It's true," piped in Puddly, "Waddler's not so bad—in fact, he's pretty nice."

"It's not only Waddler we have to contend with," answered Seeker, "it's all the other bandits on this side too. No, it wouldn't work. Grandfather's right."

"I certainly hope Grandfather has a place in mind other than our old home. The soot and ashes over there would be terrible to clean," added Tidy-Paw.

Aunt Serenity was the only one quiet, and as usual, a living picture of her name.

Seeker's reply showed his trust in Methuselah's wisdom. "Grandfather has lived many years. He'll know what to do and where to settle. He's wiser than all of us."

Precisely at that point in the conversation came Methuselah's morning whistle—a sound he had made every morning for as long as anyone could remember. He hobbled briskly over to the others gathered in the circle, bid them all "good mornin'" and sat down to breakfast. Just his happy demeanor brought cheer to the others and soon the whole atmosphere was charged with hope and excitement as they shared their simple meal. It was Posie who again raised the question.

"Well, Grandfather, where *will* we live?"

"Only The Maker knows for sure, Little Flower," he answered. "But He's given me a heap o' years, and I thought me up an idea." With that, Methuselah picked up a stick and began drawing a map in the sand at their feet.

"Now here's where we're at now—on the enemy side of the creek. And here's the other side where we used to live. We know that the wind came from the north, and this here creek put out the fire on the west side. No tellin' how far north and east she stretched—too far, I'm a-feared. But we do know how far south she's burned."

"How can you tell that, Grandfather?" asked Seeker, extremely puzzled.

"Very simple! We know, 'cause to our south lies an even wider stream than this, and 'tain't likely the fire jumped it."

"Of course, I see it now," chuckled Seeker.

"That is if my memory serves me well." Methuselah closed his eyes. "It seems to me that it runs east 'bout a day's journey south from where we are. So, let's break camp and get a-movin'."

"Aren't you forgetting one thing, Grandfather?" asked Trasher.

"What's that, Son?"

"Uprights have been spotted in that area."

"True, Son. But if it were between the Uprights and them bandits, we'd be better off a-livin' near the Uprights. We'd have to be a mite more careful—but never forget, Son, once, long ago we was friends. They've changed now, but we've never gone back on our word. We've never turned against 'em. We'll always be true to how The Maker made us—friends. We're not lookin' t'meet 'em, y'understand, but we're not their enemies, neither."

There was no more argument. When they broke camp, Furry-Ball was placed in a little vine sling on Seeker's back, while Posie walked directly behind him to see to his every need. The others took their places in line behind Methuselah and the long trip began.

At first, conversation was animated, but as the morning wore on and they grew more tired, complaints increased in number.

"Are we almost there, Grandfather?" whined Posie, stopping to pick some slightly scorched flowers for her wreath. This seemed as good as any excuse to rest. The others also stopped while she worked. She wove the wreath into a neat little circle and placed it on her head.

"Are you sure there's a stream to the south, Grandfather? How much longer 'til we get there?" begged Puddly.

"It will take hours to clean all this soot off," complained Tidy-Paw.

"Waddler saw an Upright track near here once, Grandfather," warned Trasher.

"Please, everyone, stop complaining!" complained

Seeker. As usual, Aunt Serenity said nothing, but busily filled her apron with charred acorns she found along the way. Secure in his little vine sling, Furry-Ball slept through the whole trip. Later that afternoon, Trasher and Puddly made a short reconnaissance trip to the south and returned with encouraging news.

"It's just as you said, Grandfather. The fire went only as far as the stream. If we cross it we can find a new home."

Though exhausted, they ran the last yards to the stream, arriving at sunset. How good the green forest looked to them as they crossed the stream and ate their meager supper. A large hollow log, packed with dry leaves and fir needles provided shelter for the night.

Posie curled up alongside Furry-Ball and covered him again with her tail.

"You see, Furry-Ball," she told the sleepy little ball of fur, "The Maker did provide—just as Grandfather told us He would."

Map of Methuselah's Country

CHAPTER 5

*E*xplorations

E'S GONE!" shouted Posie, waking them all up early the next morning. It was true. Furry-Ball was nowhere to be seen. Assigning partners and directions, Methuselah sent the family off to search for the little raccoon. Seeker and Puddly headed east while Tidy-Paw and Aunt Serenity back-tracked to the northern edge of the brook. Trasher and Posie went south. Methuselah himself stayed behind, just in case Furry-Ball should return. He busied himself finding food for the meal they had missed.

Posie was frantic with worry over Furry-Ball despite Methuselah's explanation of what might have happened. He had told her that when a raccoon kit was about two months old, he simply stopped sleeping and went out to meet the world. No doubt, he'd done just that and would be nearby.

Posie and Trasher had checked every hollow log and tree, but to no avail. They called and searched until their legs told them they must stop and rest. It was Posie who gave in first. "Can't we stop ahead by that pile of rocks?" she panted. And they did. But having caught their breath, they realized that this was no ordinary "pile of rocks." These rocks had been neatly stacked in an orderly way to form a barrier or wall of some sort.

"Only an Upright could have done this, Posie," said Trasher.

"Why don't we see what's on the other side, Trash—maybe he's there. Furry-Ball, I mean."

"No, he's too tiny—he couldn't have climbed over this," he assured her. "But I'll take a look. You wait here."

Posie waited for what seemed like an awfully long time while Trasher climbed to the top. "Well—I'll be . . ." he exclaimed.

"Tell me what's there," pleaded Posie.

"Just a bunch of tall stones—but they're all standing in rows and they have designs on them. And there's a big Upright house. It looks like the one Waddler told me about once."

Posie, who could never stand being an outsider, quickly clambered up alongside Trasher. "It sure is strange," she agreed. "What does it all mean, Trash?"

"Beats me!" he admitted. "But I'd say it's definitely the work of Uprights—which means we'd better get out of here quick."

With that they scurried down and agreed to return to camp, convinced that Furry-Ball *must* have been found by now. Arriving out of breath, they were relieved to find that all had returned and were gathered around Furry-Ball who had only wandered a few feet away. Methuselah had found him at the brook trying to catch a crayfish.

Very gently, Methuselah was explaining to Furry-Ball that in this family they didn't prey upon other animals or fish for food—they ate plants and vegetables instead. Furry-Ball did not seem to understand what Methuselah was saying, but he did understand the food offered to him by Tidy-Paw, and he promptly swallowed it whole. Tidy-Paw then took the baby raccoon down to the brook to teach him about cleanliness and how to wash his food. Exhausted after his fishing adventure and all the teaching that followed, Furry-Ball gave a big yawn and fell asleep right where he was.

"Breakfast is ready!" announced Methuselah.

As they gathered around the large rock table, they took turns exclaiming how hungry they were and how thoughtful it was of Methuselah to provide the food.

"'Tweren't my doin'," Methuselah reminded them. "The Maker provides it in abundance. Old Uncle Seth used to repeat the sayin', 'He gives them food in due season. He opens his hand and satisfies the desire of every living thing.'"

With that, everyone "dived in" and they were soon all eating heartily.

"How did Uncle Seth know so much about the sayings?" asked Puddly, between mouthfuls.

"He got them straight from *his* father," explained Methuselah.

"But where did they *first* come from?" Puddly persisted.

"The Maker Himself, no doubt. Why, I hear tell they're all drawn up in a Big Book—but Uncle Seth never found it. Books belong to Uprights, y'see. But he found the next best thing."

"What, Grandfather?" asked Puddly excitedly.

"The Code," he answered. "In case he ever found the Big Book, he had the Code to translate the language. Y'see, our ancestors once understood the language of the Uprights, and in order to pass it on to their children, they wrote it down on stone. For years and years they passed down this Code stone until one day Uncle Seth came upon it."

"Did you ever see it, Grandfather?" asked Puddly again.

"See it! Why—I have it!" announced Methuselah.

"But you couldn't. At least not after the fire."

"That I do," Methuselah assured him. "Y'see, while you were runnin' for your lives, I carried the Code to the place where you found me—and there I hid it! Safe and sound!"

"Can we see it?" Puddly begged.

"When there's a need for it—when the Big Book's been found," declared Methuselah. There was a moment of si-

lence as the revelation of the "Code" sank in. Then Trasher spoke.

"We saw the work of Uprights, Grandfather, when we were searching for Furry-Ball."

"And there were tall stones with drawings on them," added Posie. "Would the Code work for that?"

The Code

"Most likely not. The Big Book's what we're a-lookin' for, not tall stones," Grandfather explained. With that, he changed the subject. "In all our travels, 'twas there ever a more suitable place discovered than this for a new home?" he asked.

"I, for one, have seen nothing more favorable than this spot," said Seeker.

The others all agreed. It seemed amazing that they had found it quite by chance, when it was dark. Methuselah had already made a survey of the area and was just about to point out all the advantages when Tidy-Paw began.

"The most important thing about this place is running water, only a few feet from our door. It will help so much to keep things clean."

"The hollow stump over there will serve very well for our living area," suggested Seeker.

Puddly piped in from high above them, his voice a bit muffled. "There's a wonderful bedroom in here—big enough for us all!"

Aunt Serenity remarked, "Look at this rock here in the clearing. It's so flat! Why we couldn't ask for a better table."

Posie mentioned that the place was well-supplied with the flowers she would need for her daily wreath, and having said that, she began at once to make one.

Trasher spoke up next. "I like the way the clearing is so

protected by bushes and trees. Even the hollow stump has a hidden entrance!"

Methuselah did not need to present the results of his survey. It was already decided. They would settle here.

"In all our travels, 'twas there ever a more suitable place discovered than this for a new home?" Methuselah asked.

CHAPTER 6

The
Meeting

W E REALLY shouldn't be here," warned Posie. It was a crisp, clear autumn morning, and Puddly had convinced Posie to show him the tall stones and the big house built by the Uprights. The two had been sent to gather food for the winter, since most of their supply had been lost in the fire. On this particular food hunt they had come near the wall which Trasher and Posie had seen earlier.

"Did Grandfather ever actually forbid us to come here?" asked Puddly.

"Not exactly," answered Posie. "But he doesn't want us to have anything to do with Uprights. He says things aren't the same as they once were. He says we should have a healthy fear of them. I guess that means staying away from them, and probably their territory too."

"But he didn't say that, so it seems to me it's okay as long as we don't meet any Uprights. We'll just look at the stones and the big house. But only if it's safe," Puddly assured her.

"Okay, Puddly—but let's do it fast. I sure hope we don't meet any Uprights!"

"Don't worry. Waddler told Trasher they only come

once a week to the big house and stay for a few hours. So it's safe."

With that, Puddly scaled the wall and half slid, half jumped down the other side, with Posie following close behind. First, they investigated the tall, gray stones standing neatly in rows. Running their paws over the smooth surface of one, they discovered many different designs, all of which were a mystery to them.

"Could this be The Book that Grandfather talks so much about?" asked Posie.

"No, books aren't made of stone and they're thinner. But these designs look like the ones Grandfather says are in The Book—especially this one. Grandfather told me about one that looked just like a snake," recalled Puddly.

"You're right, Puddly, it does look a lot like a snake!" Posie could hardly contain her excitement.

The two scampered from stone to stone looking for the mysterious snake designs and puzzling over their meaning. They stopped at one where they found two of these designs on top. Very deliberately, as if to etch them permanently in their minds, they traced their paws over the marks in the stone. Absorbed as they were, they did not realize how close they had come to the big house. It was so much bigger than they had imagined. But what intrigued them most was the lovely colored pictures high above them in the walls. Below the pictures a shallow well guarded an opening made of clear stone—so clear, it looked as if they could see right through it.

"I've never seen stone you could see through before," whispered Posie excitedly. "Let's get closer to see if we can look inside." The two raccoons crept forward cautiously and pressed their noses close to the windowpane (for that's what the "clear stone" was, of course) and for a moment, they were both speechless. It was Posie who found words first.

"Oh, Puddly, did you ever see anything so beautiful? It's so lovely! And look—they don't use pine needles on the floor!"

"No, it looks just like smooth fur," Puddly observed, "but it's blue!"

"It looks *so* soft!" Posie could hardly contain herself. "Oh, look how they put sticks together, Puddly! Did you ever see so many wonderful things made out of sticks? And they are so shiny and smooth. What do you think they're for?"

"I think they sit on those," he replied, pointing to the chairs. "And that looks like our table, but it's much higher and smoother."

And then they both saw it, crying out at the same time, "A *book!*"

"Could it be The Book Grandfather told us about?" Puddly asked excitedly.

Squinting, with her nose pressed closer, Posie strained to see more. "It looks like more of those designs—yes—I think I see a snake design."

At that moment they were aware of a strange new smell, and to tell you the truth, it wasn't at all pleasant. It could best be described as a bit musty, or even rotten, not fresh and natural like the forest. Then came the sound of voices. The strange smell, combined with the sounds, could mean only one thing—Uprights! Scrambling out of the window well, they dived behind a tree for cover. The two raccoons shook as their worst fears were realized. They had almost met the Uprights, now, just a few yards away.

"Oh, I knew we shouldn't have come," whispered Posie.

"Don't worry—they won't see us," Puddly assured her. "Just stay still while I take a look." Carefully pulling a branch aside he peered around the tree. "There are two of them—one big and one little."

Posie squeezed next to him to get a clearer view. She almost forgot her fear as she gazed curiously at the first Uprights she had ever seen. Sure enough, they stood upright, but they had hardly any fur—only on the top and back of their heads. The little one's fur was especially lovely—long and gold and shiny. But, instead of having fur all over, they had smooth skin in most places. Their eyes and mouth were almost like her own. But what most intrigued Posie was what they wore (clothing and shoes). She had never seen anything like it—not even her flower wreath could match what she saw. As she thought of her wreath, she reached instinctively for it, but it was gone. In the scramble to hide, it had fallen off, and there it lay, right near the Uprights' path.

The two raccoons watched wide-eyed, as the big Up-right climbed the steps and disappeared into the big house above them. The little one walked down the path, and seeing the flower wreath, stopped and picked it up. She tried it on as she came near them. She paused, dangerously close, but then passed them and went over to a tall stone.

Posie watched breathlessly as the little Upright placed the flower wreath on the stone and sat down. Then she did an amazing thing—her fingers also traced the designs on the stone—just as Posie's and Puddly's had done minutes before. Posie decided that she and this Upright had much in common, and she liked her at once.

Meanwhile, lovely sounds could be heard coming from the big house—sounds never heard before by Posie and Puddly. They seemed to tell a story—sometimes sad, some-times joyful. When the sounds at last stopped, the small Upright bounced up and skipped off to meet the large

Upright who had come down the steps. Then the two walked away, just as they had come.

Posie and Puddly wasted no time in leaving, hoping to escape before something worse befell them. It seemed only minutes before they were safe at home, excitedly sharing their adventure with the family. Words tumbled out of their mouths like a bubbling brook, as each competed with the other to narrate the events.

After hearing the furniture described, Trasher tried to build a chair out of sticks. However, it promptly fell apart in a heap when he sat on it. Seeker then added his skill, and between the two of them, they were able to build a chair which stood the test. The others pronounced it very comfortable, and each placed an order for one just like it. Tidy-Paw seemed most interested in the description of the clear stone and imagined what a fine addition it would make to their home in the tree stump. One could certainly do a better job of cleaning, she felt sure. Aunt Serenity asked more about the beautiful sounds which told the story. She shared her belief that there were other ways besides words in which a story could be told. But it was Grandfather who seemed most interested in the description of the book. He agreed that what they described sounded like a book, but doubted whether it was The Book.

"We really didn't intend to meet the Uprights, Grandfather," assured Puddly as he ended the discussion. But one look into Grandfather's eyes, and their adventure lost some of its thrill for Posie and Puddly. They knew now what they had both known in their hearts from the start—they had been wrong to go near the Uprights' territory, even though Grandfather had not said that they shouldn't.

Methuselah

That night, Posie learned a painful lesson. In between dreams of lying on that beautiful blue rug which had looked so soft, she also saw the disappointment in Grandfather's eyes. She vowed to be true from then on, not only to what he specifically said to her, but also to that which she knew he meant. She would talk to him about it in the morning.

$\mathcal{P}$romise to Keep
A

I T WAS Methuselah's whistle that woke Posie the next morning. Quietly climbing over Furry-Ball, she hurried out to find her grandfather. The vow she had made the night before weighed heavily on her mind. How she wanted things to be the same between Grandfather and herself.

Finding him all alone, she timidly made her way over to where he was busily at work constructing something which looked an awfully lot like a chair.

"Mornin', Little Flower," he greeted her cheerfully. "I'm buildin' one of these here contraptions you saw yesterday—when you was visiting the Upright house!"

"That's what I need to talk to you about, Grandfather," she began. "You see, I knew in my heart it was wrong to go there even though you didn't *exactly* say we couldn't. And I'll never go there again, Grandfather. I'm sorry I disappointed you. And Furry-Ball—oh, Grandfather, what a bad example I was to Furry-Ball! I want to be a good example to him!" With that she began to sob.

"Now, now, Little One. I'm glad you understand that you was wrong. Sometimes our hearts understand more than our minds, Young-un." Methuselah patted Posie 'til her crying stopped.

"Grandfather, I know it's not because you hate Uprights that you don't want us to go near them. But why can't we? Will you ever change your mind?"

"No, I don't hate 'em. Remember, in The Garden we was once friends. But things is different now. They've changed—toward The Maker and toward us. In all my lifetime I haven't seen anything to prove things is different. But come to think of it, I once heard a rumor that The Maker was gonna return some day. So maybe then they will change. But for right now, I'd say they haven't changed."

"But did they *all* go against The Maker, Grandfather, everyone? Isn't there even one who still loves The Maker and us?" she questioned him. "And if there were one or two, then could we go near them and meet them, and be friends again?"

"Well, to be truthful, old Uncle Seth once told me he heard a rumor that there *was* a few Uprights who turned

Rabid and Needlenose

back to The Maker. But he never seen 'em himself. And I ain't never seen 'em either. But if there was such Uprights, we could be friends again, and there wouldn't be anyone happier than me who loves The Maker too. But you can forget ever findin' 'em, Little Flower, 'twas jest a rumor."

"Grandfather," she persisted, "if we did find them, how would we know they love The Maker like we do?"

"I s'pose by their actions," he reflected after a moment. "Jest like we show we belong to The Maker by the way we serve Him," he continued. "We do what's right. We don't steal like them other bandits—Rabid and Needlenose and the likes. And we don't go against the Uprights even when they go against us. The same goes for our brethren, even though they're our enemies—we live peaceably with everyone as best we can. And we show who we belong to by our actions toward each other. That means obeyin' the elders. But when we fail, we make it right like you jest done.

"Thank you, Little Flower. I know how sorry you feel, and I know you'll keep your promise to stay away and be a good example to Furry-Ball. And I'll keep my promise too iffen I ever find an Upright who's true to The Maker."

Posie hugged Methuselah. It was the same again with him. Then she scurried back to the log to wake up Furry-Ball.

CHAPTER 8

A
Close Call

NOW, never go farther than two tail-lengths away from me," Posie reminded Furry-Ball as they set out one crisp, cold morning.

Furry-Ball was growing bigger each day and Posie felt it her duty to be his teacher. She had begun to take him for walks, showing him how to scavenge for food and how to avoid danger. She was ever mindful now of being a good example to him and it was paying off. He constantly imitated her and she was proud of the fact that he was becoming a very obedient little brother—except for one weakness. Like Posie, he was a very inquisitive little raccoon. His reaction to all that he learned was to ask, "Why?" It was no different this particular morning.

"I'm big enough to take care of myself," he assured her. "So, *why* do I always have to stay near you?"

"Because something dangerous might happen, Furry-Ball. Promise you'll obey me?"

"Okay," he agreed grudgingly.

Posie was looking for a few dried flowers to make her daily wreath, but even dried flowers were becoming more scarce as winter drew nearer. As a last resort, she and Furry-Ball approached the stone wall area. Posie remembered a late-blooming goldenrod patch near there. This time, however, she vowed that they wouldn't go over the wall—they would only pick the flowers near it. She enlisted Furry-Ball in the search and soon they had gathered almost enough for a wreath. Sitting down, Posie began work on her masterpiece, intently weaving each stem behind and under the others. She loved this part best, and turned it into an art as she improved her skill each day. All the other family members commented on her artistic talent when she made an especially beautiful or different wreath. This day's work would bring many comments, she was sure. So totally engrossed was she in her task, that she did not see Furry-Ball stray farther and farther away—much farther than the two tail-lengths he had promised her just a short while before.

As he approached the wall, an especially large, dried goldenrod waved enticingly from the other side. He looked quickly at Posie, and seeing her absorbed in her work, lost no time in squeezing through a tiny opening in the stones at the bottom of the wall. Once on the other side, however, he forgot his mission entirely as he gazed in wonder at the large Upright building ahead of him. Could that glitter near the bottom of the big house be the clear stone which Posie and Puddly had mentioned? He ran over and jumped down into the small well around the clear stone opening. All that Posie and Puddly had said was true. It was fascinating to look through the clear stone. Suddenly he remembered his promise to Posie, and he knew that he must return at once. But it was too late. He could not seem to get a foothold on the sides of the smooth walls of the well and he was too tiny to jump high enough to escape. He squealed with fright, as he tried again and again to climb out. Now he knew that Posie had been right and how he wished he had listened to her.

His squeals brought an immediate reaction—but not

from Posie. While she scurried on her side of the wall frantically searching for her little brother, a small Upright face
on the other side of the clear stone opening looked out in
amazement at the frightened little raccoon. Meanwhile, Posie, having heard Furry-Ball's cries, climbed a tree to look
over the wall, and saw the dangerous situation facing
Furry-Ball. Terrified, she realized the decision she now had
to make—to disobey Methuselah in order to save her little
brother. Yet somehow she knew that this was the *right* thing
to do—as if The Maker Himself were telling her to go and
save him.

She caught only a fleeting glimpse of the face at the
window, but it was enough to bring to her memory the

features of the little Upright she had seen several weeks before. Posie had instantly taken a liking to her, yet she had no assurance that this little Upright felt the same way about her. Without hesitation, Posie raced down the tree, over the wall and darted toward the well where Furry-Ball was trapped. The face had disappeared, but reappeared just as Posie reached the edge of the well.

Then everything happened so quickly that Posie could scarcely remember what came first. She called to Furry-Ball to grab hold of her tail which she swung down into the well. At almost the same time the window opened, and an Upright hand appeared dangerously close to Furry-Ball who was trembling from head to tail. In the hand was something long and thin, circled with red and white stripes. All this Posie saw out of the corner of her eye, but her nose gave her a better description. Suddenly she was conscious of the most tantalizing aroma she had ever smelled, filling the air around her, and she knew the object in the hand was food. Could this be the Upright bait she had heard Methuselah tell Trasher and Puddly about? Posie saw Furry-Ball's nose twitch with eagerness as he caught this delicious scent. The fur on her body stood on end, and she heard herself screaming with an urgency she had never felt before—"No, Furry-Ball, No!"

Shocked into action, Furry-Ball obeyed her warning. With one motion, he leaped up and grabbed Posie's tail and in a split second was out of the well. Not only did he stay within two tail-lengths, but he almost climbed over his big sister as they raced between the tall stones and toward the wall. In the course of their flight, Posie's flower wreath slid off, and though aware of her loss, she never stopped. She knew that saving a life was her first priority. She never looked back until the silence behind her made her aware that Furry-Ball had stopped running.

Realizing they were well out of sight, she let Furry-Ball rest and catch his breath. When at last they were breathing normally again, a badly shaken Furry-Ball spoke first.

"I should have listened to you, Posie," he admitted. "I'm glad you came and helped me. I'll obey from now on!" And it was clear that he meant it.

Furry-Ball

"That's okay," said Posie, much relieved. "I forgive you. But we *will* have to tell Grandfather."

"I know," Furry-Ball agreed sadly.

And they did. Posie hoped Methuselah would understand about her decision to disobey as she tried to describe the voice inside her.

"I've never heard the voice of The Maker before like you have, Grandfather," she said. "It wasn't a loud voice, but I think it was *His* voice. I felt sorry to disobey you—but more afraid not to obey Him."

"You did the proper thing, Little Flower. It was The Maker's voice you heard, all right."

It was a very remorseful Furry-Ball who drifted off to sleep that night, but he was especially thankful for Posie's soft furry tail which not only covered him then, but had saved his life that very day.

Posie lay awake for a long time. She felt overwhelmed with the realization that The Maker had at last spoken to her, and she was glad that she had listened to His voice. Though she had never spoken to The Maker before, she timidly whispered a quiet little "Thank you" to Him and at last fell asleep.

CHAPTER 9

The Gift

NO ONE seemed to notice that for several days Posie had not been wearing her customary wreath. They were seated around the breakfast table enjoying Aunt Serenity's sun-dried blueberries gathered from across the brook, when Methuselah spoke up.

"Speakin' of enjoyin' The Maker's gifts, 'taint often we see you without your daily wreath, Little Flower. In fact, it's been a while since we last saw one. Gettin' too old I s'pose, are you?"

"No, Grandfather, I'll never grow too old for flowers—it's just that . . ." she broke off as a tear trickled down her cheek.

"Now, now, child—whatever's a-botherin' you can be fixed up in no time—just tell us all what's wrong."

"It's gone—that's what's wrong, Grandfather." Another tear trickled down. "My winter wreath, I mean . . . and it was so beautiful! It fell off when Furry-Ball and I were running away from the Upright a few days ago." More tears streamed down. And now tears could be seen on Furry-Ball's cheeks too.

"Now, now, Little One—we'll jest get a-goin' and find some more flowers and make a new one in no time."

Before she knew it, Posie, Methuselah and Furry-Ball were off on a search for dried flowers. Her tears were soon forgotten as they discovered fine patches of dried goldenrod and Queen Anne's lace. They were chatting back and forth merrily as they gathered, when one of Posie's flowers dropped into a crevice behind a rock. Using her agile little fingers to retrieve it, she felt something smooth and hard and round. She grasped it firmly, pulled it out, and brushed off the dirt.

Her mouth fell open in amazement. It was a circular band of gold! Never had she seen anything like it. Often she had found smooth pebbles, stones that glittered or round rocks—but never anything like this. As her fingers felt the smooth band of gold, a small clump of dirt fell off revealing something even more startling. Two snake-like designs were engraved on the inside of the band. Posie knew this could only mean one thing—the circular band must belong to an Upright.

In the midst of her excitement, a question came to her mind—what should she do with it? Always before she had kept each treasure she had found—shiny stones, empty snail shells, pretty flowers—but this was different. Here was a band of gold that belonged to an Upright. The designs proved that. Somehow they seemed familiar to her. Then she remembered. These designs were exactly the same as those she had seen on the tall stone beyond the wall.

Could there be some connection between that stone and the band of gold? How mysterious it all seemed. One part of her wanted to return the treasure—but to whom, and how? The other part of her longed to keep it. Surely she could think of something lovely to make with it. Before she could make a decision, however, Furry-Ball interrupted her.

"Do we have enough yet, Posie? I'm tired of picking flowers."

"Yes," she answered him. "But wait over there—I'll be there in a minute." With that, she secretly dropped the band down into the crevice and pushed the rock back into place. Now it was safe, and no one knew but her. Relieved, she joined the others and added her flowers to the pile.

"Told you not to worry, Young-un—The Maker always provides more than enough—iffen we do our part a-lookin'," said Methuselah.

Posie couldn't help smiling at the thought of what The Maker had provided in addition to the flowers. But then she realized again that the band of gold didn't really belong to her. All the way home she tossed the problem back and forth in her mind—should she keep it or return it? Finally she decided to ask Methuselah for guidance.

"Grandfather, if you found something that belonged to someone—but you didn't know who—would you have to return it?"

"The Maker requires us to be honest, Little Flower. He is Himself, you see," he replied. "And as to returnin' it when you don't rightly know whose it is—why He can get right into your thinkin' and give you ideas you never realized you had."

Posie knew he was right, but she wasn't sure how The Maker could help her find the owner. Yet He had spoken to her once. Maybe He would speak again.

At last they were home. No sooner had the little band taken their seats to watch Posie weave her wreath, when Puddly and Trasher arrived with news.

"Guess what we found, Posie and Furry-Ball?" they shouted. Without waiting for a response, they presented her with the very flower wreath she had lost several days before. Her eyes widened as she realized the great risk her brothers had taken for her.

"Thank you!" she whispered with gratitude, clasping

*"With that, she secretly dropped the band down into the crevice
and pushed the rock back into place."*

her work of art. "But you shouldn't have gone—it was too dangerous! Where did you find it?"

"On our side of the wall," answered Trasher. "It was hanging on a branch."

"But that's not all," added Puddly. "We found something else with it."

"What?" asked Furry-Ball, fairly twitching with curiosity. They all gathered around as Puddly opened his hand. A tantalizing smell filled the air and Posie recognized it to be the same red and white object that had been in the small Upright's hand during the attempt to rescue Furry-Ball.

Methuselah was carefully examining it when Trasher interrupted, "And we found something else too!" he announced. "This." He took from his yellow scarf something smooth, white, flat and as thin as a leaf. There on it were the unmistakable Upright designs they had seen before. They stared at the curious marks in silence, and then Posie gasped. She recognized two snake designs at the bottom of

the white object, detached from the other designs. They all turned to look at her as she tried to explain her discovery.

"These two snake designs are exactly the same as two we saw on one of the tall stones," she explained. ("And the same as on the band of gold," she thought to herself.)

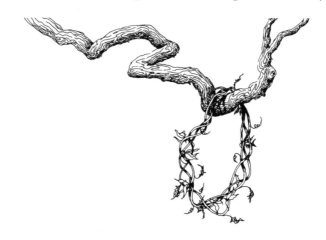

"Maybe it's some kind of message," Puddly said.

For the rest of the evening around the supper table, they discussed the event—trying to make some sense of it. They concluded that the small Upright had found the wreath and placed it on a branch along with the red and white food and a message, and that it was undoubtedly a gift to Posie. But why, they didn't know. If only they knew the meaning of the designs. Finally Methuselah put an end to their discussion with his startling announcement.

"Tomorrow we'll go get the Code," he promised. "It jest might shed some light on things a bit. It 'pears to me to be the same kind of designs as those on the Code."

Posie had great difficulty sleeping that night. She knew now that The Maker had indeed spoken again to her and given her the idea that the band of gold might belong to the small Upright whose designs were on the message and also on the tall stone. *But what did the message say?* she wondered. *Could the red and white food really be a gift to her?* It smelled so good—she longed to take a nibble or even a tiny lick. But she dared not—especially when she thought of the band of gold hidden beneath the rock. How could she accept the Upright's gift when she herself was hiding a treasure that probably belonged to the Upright? If the Upright knew she was hiding the gold band, she probably wouldn't have given her this gift. She felt so unworthy and guilty.

Then at last, the answer came to her. She would return the band of gold to her new friend. It would be her gift to the small Upright. How, she didn't know—but she would. Posie fell asleep with this thought.

$\mathcal{T}$eamwork

I T WAS still dark when Methuselah's whistle broke the
early morning silence. Everyone rubbed sleepy eyes and
stretched. Then, remembering the important mission
for the day, they hurried down to breakfast.

Aunt Serenity, Trasher and Puddly bustled about preparing food for the excited family while the others waited
eagerly for word from Methuselah as to how they would
carry out their mission.

"When can we go, Grandfather?" asked Puddly.

"Now, don't be a–rushin' us, Puddly," chided Methuselah. "It's mighty risky goin' back to the old homestead.
There's no protection there now since the fire. We'll need
to think us up a plan for bringin' the Code here safe." He
and Seeker walked a few paces away talking quietly while
the others waited impatiently, getting more restless by the
minute.

To make the delay even more unbearable, Aunt Serenity
announced that breakfast was ready. They all sat down to
eat and literally bolted down their food. That was, all but
Methuselah and Aunt Serenity. They calmly discussed the
weather and ate slowly, savoring each bite, much to the
dismay of the rest.

After what seemed an endless wait, Methuselah spoke. "We'll need everyone's help iffen we aim to bring the Code here safe. We can't afford for anyone to find out we have it. We owe it to Uncle Seth and those after him, who kept it safe all these years. There's a right good chance of meetin' them outlaws seein' as there's such a shortage of food. I've heard tell they're havin' to come out in the day, jest to find enough to eat. And since there's so few trees, there's a good chance of bein' seen."

Puddly

Methuselah then carefully described each family member's responsibility. Seeker and he would go directly to the rock enclosure and carry out the Code, concealing it with leaves. Trasher and Puddly would skirt their old area and distract any enemy who seemed headed in the direction of Methuselah and Seeker. The rest would go about their daily business—gathering food around their new home—in order not to arouse their enemies' suspicion.

All received their orders willingly except for Puddly. He seemed put out at having what he considered a minor part in the mission. "I wanted to help carry the Code," he complained.

"In accomplishin' a mission, no team member's job is too little, Puddly," reminded Methuselah. "The Maker sees all the same and all jobs the same. 'Twas only after the Uprights left The Maker that them and us stopped doin' our job. But not all of us, Puddly. And I know you'll be on the team with all the rest of us—I'm a-countin' on you to do your job."

Puddly did not look particularly convinced as the small band started out after breakfast. It was windy and cold, and dark clouds made them realize it would get even colder. They walked briskly, but did not run for fear of attracting attention. Upon reaching the brook which divided their old area from enemy territory, they separated. Methuselah and Seeker went to get the Code while Puddly and Trasher stayed at the brook to distract their enemies. No sooner had Methuselah and Seeker left than Trasher suggested, "You stay down here by the brook, Puddly, while I go to the top of the hill and hide behind that old burned out log—in case I have to warn Grandfather and Father." With that, he turned and scooted up the hill and behind the log.

Puddly didn't even get a chance to argue back before he heard noises. To his dismay, several of their enemies were moving toward him on the opposite side of the brook. Instead of wondering if his job were too small, now he began to feel that maybe it was too big for him. Inwardly, he cringed at the sight of the leader of their enemies—Rabid himself. Needlenose accompanied him along with Slinky and Raider. Waddler lagged behind as usual. Rising to the occasion, Puddly greeted them politely.

"Thinkin' of changin' sides, eh, Boy?" challenged Needlenose with a sneer. "Ain't enough food over there, so you're thinkin' of comin' over to our side, eh?" They all laughed.

"No, as a matter of fact, we've got plenty of food. I was just out for a walk," answered Puddly.

"Likely story, Boy." Rabid emphasized "Boy" with a contemptuous snarl. "Come on over here and tell us what you're *really* up to."

Out of the corner of his eye, Puddly saw Trasher slip out of sight. He knew he'd gone to warn Methuselah and Seeker. He also knew he'd have to stall for time before he got help.

"I'd be glad to talk to you from here," he answered politely. "As I said, I'm just out for a walk—I sure miss this place." Looking straight at Waddler, he continued, "Say,

Waddler, do you remember the splash fights we used to have here in the brook before the fire?"

Everyone turned as Waddler nodded.

"I *always* used to win, didn't I, Waddler?"

"Did not," denied Waddler.

"Did too," Puddly argued back.

"Well, let's see if you can win this time, you little runt," challenged Needlenose. "A little water never hurt anyone," he added. The others all agreed.

Puddly had not planned on a splash fight. The clouds were darker than ever, and the wind had picked up. He knew he'd be chilled to the bone after a water fight, but he also knew the others were depending on him to do his part. So, without hesitation, he boldly stepped into the brook and splashed Waddler first.

Stunned, Waddler stood there for a moment and then returned the splash. Puddly knew he could make short work

of the clumsy Waddler, but he also knew that he had to somehow drag out the battle. He purposely missed Waddler on occasion and let him get the edge now and then. This delighted the rest who cheered from the sidelines. Puddly began to feel sorry for Waddler who had been pushed into this fight by the others. He made sure that more and more of his splashes reached them. This strategy worked, and before long they were fairly well soaked and shivering along with Waddler.

It was Rabid who allowed as how they'd "better quit this game playin'" and "get on with food huntin'." And with that they ambled off.

Puddly knew very well that Rabid was inwardly weak and very selfish. Like most bullies, he couldn't "take it" and called it quits only because he himself was cold. In a moment they were out of sight, and Puddly felt safer. He hadn't realized how cold he was. If only he were home under a warm blanket of leaves and pine needles, he thought as he turned away from the brook. Startled, he looked up to see Methuselah, Seeker, and Trasher all rushing down the hill toward him.

"You did it, Son, and the Code's safe!" Methuselah said proudly.

"But, I'm so cold!" shivered Puddly.

Without a word, the three lifted him up, placed him on a makeshift stretcher and covered him with dry leaves. How good that felt to Puddly. Soon the warmth reached him and his shivering stopped. As they headed home with Seeker carrying the front and Trasher and Methuselah together taking the back end of the stretcher, Puddly felt something hard and smooth next to him. He knew that Methuselah and Seeker had done their job—this must be the Code.

The little band arrived home safely with their treasure and Trasher eagerly related Puddly's adventures. Aunt Serenity and Tidy-Paw busied themselves with making a warm bed of dry straw and leaves for Puddly. Furry-Ball and Posie had something to share too. They had also encountered some of the enemy while scrounging for food. Clutcher, Rubbish and Stealer had come along on the other side of the brook and had asked if they had any food on that side. Furry-Ball had directed them to a dead fish he had seen further down on their side. His quick thinking averted a confrontation and they passed on without incident.

That night, Seeker and Trasher dug a pit to hide the Code, covering it with a large rock slab. That in turn they covered with leaves. Their job was done—they had accomplished their mission! They had worked successfully as a team. But the happiest team member of all was Puddly. How glad he was that he had done his job.

CHAPTER 11

For
You

WINTER was here. A bitter cold wind swept through the forest, leaving all that it touched with a covering of snow. A stray snowflake blew right through the doorway and landed on Furry-Ball's nose, waking him from a sound sleep. It was wet and cold and something he had never seen or felt before. Peeking through the doorway, he could hardly believe his eyes. The green forest was no longer green—it was covered with a white blanket. It looked so inviting that he climbed out of the hole and down the tree. "Help" came his muffled cry from deep within a snowdrift. His cry awoke the others and brought Seeker to his rescue. Moments later a panic-stricken Furry-Ball emerged from the snowdrift as Seeker dug him out.

"I don't like this!" was Furry-Ball's first remark. "Besides—it's very cold!" This brought laughter from the others who were watching the two from above.

"It's not safe to go out for food," Seeker reported. "We'd better wait for the snow to melt a bit. It's much too deep."

Aunt Serenity encouraged them all by announcing, "We have a small emergency food supply hidden in the wall of this very room." Sure enough, in just minutes she had a delightful spread of food before them. As they ate breakfast in their cozy corner they gave thanks to The Maker for Aunt Serenity's amazing resourcefulness.

"It's all from Him, you know," she reminded them, "including the idea to hide some food here."

Posie pricked up her ears. "So, The Maker speaks to Aunt Serenity through ideas too," she thought to herself.

After breakfast, Seeker talked with Methuselah about the possibility of going for the Code. "The snow's too deep for a long trip, but I think we could make it to the pit and back with the Code—it's not too far. It would be worth a try, anyway. We're stuck here because of the storm so we might as well make some use of the time to translate that document the boys found."

It was agreed. Seeker, Trasher and Puddly set off in the deep snow. Soon they were out of sight, and completely swallowed up by the blinding whiteness. Those in the shelter turned away from their vigil at the door and tried not to worry about the dangers facing their loved ones.

Furry-Ball voiced all their concern by observing, "They seem so alone out there!"

"That they do," agreed Methuselah, "'cept for one thing."

"What's that, Grandfather?" Furry-Ball questioned him.

"The Maker's out there with them," reminded Methuselah.

"But can *He* help them?" asked Furry-Ball searchingly.

"Yep—The Maker's right there to help—givin' 'em ideas so's they can find their way home," he said encouragingly.

Furry-Ball seemed relieved and scurried over to Posie who was busily weaving something from straw. He watched intently and then tried to follow her example.

Hours passed. At last came the sounds of the voices they were waiting to hear.

"Seeker, Trasher and Puddly set off in the deep snow. Soon they were out of sight, swallowed up by the blinding whiteness."

"They're back!" shouted Furry-Ball excitedly.

A cheer went up from the others as they greeted the returning adventurers. It took all of them to lift and pull the heavy stone into their shelter. Once it was inside, they examined it carefully, taking turns to decipher its meaning. "You might as well quit tryin'," laughed Methuselah. "Old Uncle Seth gave me the key to understandin' it and it's right here in my head!"

"So you *do* know what it means, then, Grandfather?" asked Trasher, expectantly.

"That I do," he answered, "and as soon as we can clear us a corner, your father and I will use the Code to find the meanin' of this here document."

Carefully smoothing out the white leaf, he placed it alongside the Code. Then Methuselah and Seeker sat down and, talking in quiet tones, began the task of translation.

Time seemed to drag on endlessly. Night fell. Morning dawned. Another night came, and still another day passed while the storm continued to rage outside their shelter. Puddly, Trasher, Posie and Furry-Ball were becoming increasingly bored. They had played all the inside games they knew and longed to go outside and play. The snow was now so deep that even to go to the bottom of the tree would be dangerous. Aunt Serenity had come to the end of her food supply that night and they all knew they would have to face the next day on empty stomachs.

How thankful they all were the next morning to wake up to blue skies again, and no wind. Yet they still could not leave the safety of their shelter until the snow began to melt.

"It's my turn!" "No, it's *mine!*" The children argued over who could look out the door next.

Even Tidy-Paw and Aunt Serenity were struggling with housecleaning chores and everyone was in the way. Methuselah and Seeker settled down in their corner again as they continued translating the document. Then, when irritability and boredom had reached their peak, a shout was heard above all the other noises.

"We've got it!" It was Seeker who stood and waved the document as they all pressed in close to hear what he said. "Grandfather, since it was largely your work, why don't you give the translation of the document?" he suggested.

"What does it say?" they all asked in unison.

It got very quiet as a broad grin spread over Methuselah's face. "It says simply, 'For you!'" he announced.

"For you?" they again asked in unison.

"That's all?" asked Trasher.

"All 'ceptin the name at the end, and we know it's the 'zact same name as that seen by Posie and Puddly on the tall stone."

"So it *was* a gift for Posie," exclaimed Furry-Ball. "I knew it was!" he shouted, jumping up and down.

Everyone turned to look at Posie, but she was back by her bed uncovering something. She came over to them all and held up the red and white object.

"Since it's mine," she began, "I want to share it with all of you. I know you're all hungry." She gave it to Methuselah to divide. As he broke it into pieces, a delicious smell filled the room. Eating it very slowly so as to enjoy every bite, they all agreed that never had they tasted anything so good. How thankful they were to the little Upright for this special gift. It was not only a delicious treat, but it had also been their only food for the day.

That night, Posie told the family about the golden band she had found and her desire to give it as a gift to her new friend. "It's only right," they all agreed. "But how can this be done?" they wondered.

Posie already had an idea—right from The Maker Himself, she was sure. She was lying awake in her bed thinking about the little Upright. *Even though I can't speak her language,*

I now know how to write two of her words. If only I could write them on something, I could leave a letter with the golden band on the tall stone. She'd surely find it there. But how can I write? I don't have anything to write with and I don't even have a white leaf. With these thoughts whirling round and round in her mind, she fell asleep.

CHAPTER 12

P.Mud
rints

PLEASE wipe the mud off your feet before coming in, Furry, Dear," Tidy-Paw reminded him for the third time that morning.

Several warm days had replaced the melting snow with a sea of mud. The family had been busy bringing food from their supply closets hidden nearby in the forest. This meant much extra cleaning for Tidy-Paw each time one of them came in. Posie couldn't remember how often her mother had reminded them to wipe their feet. There seemed to be mud all over. Suddenly it came to her! Mud! Of course! That was it! That was the answer to her dilemma. She could write with mud!

Posie's thoughts turned back to the day before when Grandfather had accompanied her to the spot where she had hidden the golden band. Carefully, they had removed the rock and found it exactly as she had left it.

She remembered how Methuselah had stared at the two snake designs on the golden band. "The same as them on the document," he had confirmed.

"But how can I return it, Grandfather, without writing her a letter? And how can I write a letter when I don't have anything to write with or on? I do so want her to know that it's from me. And I wish I could tell her I received her gift too," Posie had said wistfully. "Do you think she serves The Maker like we do—is that why she gave me a gift?"

"I'll be a-forgettin' all your questions, Little Flower, iffen you don't slow down a mite," Methuselah had interrupted. "We have to come at this thing mighty cautious-like. True, we know that an Upright, probably the one you met by the name of 'S.S.,' gave you a gift—but we don't know why. Both you and I want to believe that it's 'cause of followin' The Maker that made her do it. But we need to be mighty careful not to jump to any conclusions. Now as to what to write on, Little Flower, the answer's plain and clear—the other side of the document!"

"Grandfather, I never even thought of that! What a wonderful idea!"

"And since the little Upright wrote on one side, you'll be a-lettin' her know you received her letter and gift at the same time," Methuselah had added.

"You're right, Grandfather—she'll know! Now all I need is something to write with."

Tidy-Paw's scolding of Furry-Ball brought Posie back to the present. "Furry-Ball, you're leaving mud prints all over!"

"That's it!" she said out loud. "Thank you, Furry-Ball, for leaving mud prints all over—that's just what I'll use! I'll write with mud prints!"

The whole family looked up at once, shocked and surprised—especially Tidy-Paw.

"Well, I didn't mean *that* exactly," explained Posie. "I meant that Furry-Ball's mud prints gave me an idea. That's how I'll write a letter to the Upright!" she announced.

"I never thought I'd see the day when mud prints had value!" sighed Tidy-Paw as she hugged Furry-Ball who glowed with a feeling of accomplishment. No one could hide a smile.

"Yes, indeed," admitted Methuselah. "The Maker Himself could not have come up with a better idea than writin' with mud prints!"

Posie smiled. She was sure that the idea *had* come from The Maker Himself. "And if I use the other side of her letter, she'll know I got her gift," added Posie excitedly. "I'll leave it on the tall stone where we first saw her. I just know she'll find it!"

It was settled. Tidy-Paw herself supervised the task of mixing a big scoop of mud on her clean table. The whole family watched as Posie practiced writing the message on the ground first. Then, very carefully, she placed her paw in the mud, and turning the document over, formed the same designs the Upright had made—"FOR YOU!" The whole family held their breath, for fear that Posie would make a mistake. But when the letter was finished and compared to the Upright's, they all agreed it was a job well done. They took turns blowing on it, hoping the mud would dry more quickly. But it was Seeker who finally suggested that they leave it in the sun and perhaps by the next day it would be ready to deliver.

Morning could not come quickly enough for Posie. She had plucked the most beautiful dried flower from her wreath and intended to poke it through the bottom of the letter for her signature. (Because, of course, she did not know how to write her name.) This gave her another idea. With so much experience in weaving wreaths, she could also weave several strands of straw together to make a chain and attach the golden band to the letter by poking the chain through the paper in the same way.

She was up before breakfast working diligently on her idea. By the time Methuselah was awake, Posie was able to show him the finished product.

"A right good job, Little Flower," he complimented her.

"Grandfather, I think the ideas came from The Maker, just as you said they would," suggested Posie. "They just popped right into my head when I needed them."

"I've known The Maker for many a year, and He's never let me down once when it's ideas I've a-needed," confessed Methuselah.

At breakfast, the family discussed who would go with Posie to return the golden band. Finally Trasher was selected. They knew he would make sure it was safe before venturing into Upright territory.

The trip was uneventful except for the surge of joy in Posie's heart when she finally placed the letter with the golden band on the tall stone. How good it felt to do the right thing, and by doing it, give her new friend a surprise. Trasher and Posie climbed a tree on the other side of the stone wall and watched for a long time, but no one came. They decided then to return home, but to come back each day to see if the gift had been taken.

Puddly took his turn the following day along with Posie, but still nothing had been taken.

By the third day, Furry-Ball was allowed to go, since he promised he would not go past the wall. As they were almost ready to leave their hiding place in the tree, they heard familiar sounds—Upright voices! Posie's fur stood on end in anticipation as she and Furry-Ball watched the Uprights approach the big house. The large Upright climbed up the steps and went into the building, and soon lovely sounds came forth.

At the same time, the small Upright skipped over to the tall stone. As she placed her fingers on the snake designs, she caught sight of the gift Posie had left for her. Excitedly she grabbed the letter. Posie would never forget the look on her face as she read it. How surprised and pleased she seemed! In fact, she gave a little squeal of delight as she saw the golden band. Posie watched her loosen it from the letter and then slip it onto her finger. "So that's what it's for," she thought. And then, almost in one motion, the Upright hugged the letter to her heart and ran into the big house. Shortly after, Posie and Furry-Ball saw the two Uprights leave, the same way they had come. Posie and Furry-Ball left too. They could hardly wait to tell the rest of the family.

$\mathcal{H}$elp

B E SURE to cover your tracks, Furry-Ball" reminded Trasher one cold, wintry day. Furry-Ball was now big enough to be of help to the family, and so he had begun to go along with Trasher to bring back food from their hidden pantry in the forest. Trasher, his yellow scarf gallantly trailing from his neck, and ever concerned with secrecy, was training him in the art of track-covering.

"But why, Trasher?" came Furry-Ball's persistent question.

"Because there are some bandits nearby who will steal all our food if we don't keep our hiding place secret," Trasher explained.

"You mean Needlenose and Waddler?" asked Furry-Ball.

"Well, Needlenose for sure," answered Trasher, "but I don't think Waddler would. He just follows the rest of the bandits because they feed him—but I think he likes us too." Trasher checked Furry-Ball's work. "If you ever come here alone, Furry-Ball, don't forget to do this. We don't have a very big food supply this year because of the fire, so don't ever forget," he warned. The two returned from the hidden pantry with their bundles of food, which Tidy-Paw and Aunt Serenity prepared for dinner.

Meanwhile, Methuselah and Seeker continued their study of the Code. Methuselah had been teaching Seeker how to translate the Upright symbols into raccoon language when he noticed that Trasher, Puddly and Posie were listening intently close by. "Why don't you young-uns gather round here and learn something," he said. The children crowded in excitedly. Not wanting to disturb them, Tidy-Paw quietly enlisted Furry-Ball to run an errand for her.

"Please run back and fetch a few more nuts, Dear," she requested.

Furry-Ball was excited about going on an errand alone, and dashed off to the pantry in the woods. He had managed to borrow Trasher's scarf for the occasion as he thought it would help him remember to cover his tracks the way Trasher had told him to do. But just before he entered the hollow log and was about to reach for the nuts, the wind blew something white, right past his nose. He quickly grabbed the nuts and chased after the white object, finally seizing it with his paw. His excitement mounted when he made a startling discovery. "Why, this is just like that white leaf we found before! But this one is not flat and smooth; it's all crumpled up," he thought. Still, feeling it had value, he carefully tucked it in the scarf, next to the nuts. He was sure his family would be happy to see this when he got home.

And what excitement Furry-Ball's white leaf did bring. Since Methuselah had brought back the Code, the whole family had made progress learning the meaning of the symbols and how to write them. They had been using their paws to practice in the mud around their home. Sometimes, when Tidy-Paw was preoccupied, the children would even practice on the table and quickly wipe it off before she noticed. Furry-Ball's white leaf meant that they could write another document or letter, so they continued to practice their writing. Although they did not yet know to whom they should write or when, they decided to hide the white leaf in their living room for some special use in the future. Finding just the spot, they carefully buried their treasure and retired to bed.

Early the next morning, Trasher's shouts awakened them.

"It's gone—it's *all* gone!" he cried.

"What's gone?" Tidy-Paw asked, with alarm.

"Our food supply—all of it!" answered Trasher. "Someone didn't cover his tracks and those bandits found it!"

All eyes turned toward Furry-Ball, for he'd been the last one to get food. "I forgot," he admitted, and he began to sob.

"May The Maker preserve us," said Tidy-Paw as the reality of their loss set in.

The conversation that followed was what you would expect under the circumstances. There was much accusing and blaming. "If only you had been more careful," and "Why didn't you cover your tracks," and "I told you so." But Aunt Serenity's words of comfort to Furry-Ball put an end to their bickering.

"There, there," she said softly, "now it's not *all* gone."

"It's not?" they all asked in unison.

"Why, of course not," she said calmly. "I always lay up a little extra for emergencies—but, mind you, it's not enough to get us through the winter. Knowin' The Maker, though, He'll provide for us—just like He provided a new home when we needed it."

"That He did," affirmed Methuselah. "It's up to us to do our part, though. That means every day, all the men folk searchin' for food—even if it's not 'xactly to our likin'. But when we've run out of that, The Maker will provide jest like Aunt Serenity says. He's done it for us before."

Furry-Ball was the first to respond. "Since it's all my fault that our food is gone, I'll start right now to look for some more, Grandfather."

"Maybe Trasher and I could just cross the brook and find those bandits and *make* them give us our food back," suggested Puddly.

"Yer all makin' a big fuss about nothin' at all," answered Methuselah. "First of all, we'll gather our food from the emergency pantry 'til it's gone and at the same time be a-gatherin' each day what we can find. And, as to takin' our food back from those bandits, we gotta remember they're hungry too and they don't know The Maker like we do. Stealin's the only way they know."

There was no further discussion. Trasher went to Aunt

Serenity's emergency pantry and determined that they had several weeks of food left if they used it sparingly. Each day, they went out to search for overlooked food. It was amazing how they all learned to eat less and even to *like* foods that they had disliked before.

While on one of these food-gathering expeditions, Furry-Ball and Posie found themselves once again very close to the wall. Furry-Ball cast a remembering glance toward the spot where he and Posie had climbed over to escape the Upright. All of a sudden, a slight movement caught his eye. At the same time, his nostrils picked up a delicious scent. It was then that he saw it—a hand, holding a shiny, red apple! And right behind the wall, a little face that was now familiar to them both—it was the little girl Upright!

"Look!" yelled Furry-Ball.

Posie stopped in her tracks. She was not afraid, just startled. She studied the little Upright's expression for a moment—her wide eyes and upturned mouth seemed to communicate friendliness. Posie wished so much she could talk to her in her own language. How she wanted to tell her that she was her friend. She was about to turn away when she noticed the little Upright's hand extending over the wall with the apple. Was she imagining it, or was the little Upright offering her the apple? Before she could decide, Furry-Ball stepped forward. The little Upright's hand moved toward him. Posie moved instinctively to protect her little brother. With that, the Upright's other hand came over the wall holding another apple. The delicious smell was almost overpowering.

Furry-Ball broke the silence. "I think she wants us to take them," he whispered. "Can't we?"

Posie thought about this. They had received a gift from her before, so why not now, she reasoned. "Let *me* go first,"

"Was she imagining it, or was the little Upright offering her an apple?"

she answered, "and if anything happens, you run as fast as you can, Furry-Ball!"

She took one step forward and the hand moved nearer too. This continued until Posie could just about reach out and touch the apple. She held her breath. A wonderful feeling of trust came over her as she reached out her paws. Closer and closer she moved them toward the apple. She grabbed it, and it was hers! Holding it tightly she signaled Furry-Ball to do the same. As soon as the two raccoons had their paws on the apples, the little Upright hands moved back behind the wall, making that little waving gesture which they had seen once before.

At last Posie understood. "This means something friendly," she thought. Overwhelmed with the desire to communicate, she put down her apple and raised her paw in the same way. Furry-Ball followed her example.

They ran home as fast as they could, and placing the apples on the table, blurted out the story of how they had gotten them. Their food supply was dangerously low and this gift would be of great help to them. How good these fresh apples tasted, making dinner very special that night, and when it was over, all that remained were the seeds, which Furry-Ball kept.

The family drifted off to sleep rather quickly, but Furry-Ball could not sleep. He lay awake thinking. How he wished he had not left his tracks uncovered. He had to think of a way to find more food. And then suddenly he had the answer—those seeds he'd saved—the apple seeds— they came from the Upright. Maybe she could help. Quietly, he tip-toed out of bed to Methuselah.

Gently tapping him with his paw, he asked, "Grandfather, could you help me write a letter tomorrow, on the white leaf I found?"

"Iffen I ever get some sleep, I will, Son. Now why don't you go back to bed and we'll talk about it in the mornin'."

Furry-Ball obeyed, but early the next morning, he was up sharing his plan with Methuselah. After breakfast, Methuselah gathered the family together and told them of Furry-Ball's plan.

It took several days of study and translation, but the day finally came when Posie could write their finished work on the white leaf. When the writing was completed, Furry-Ball himself went with Trasher and placed the document on the wall where they had met the Upright. And on top of the document, he carefully placed the apple seeds that he'd saved.

The two raccoons were hardly out of sight when the little Upright appeared and discovered the white paper with the apple seeds on top. Picking it up, she read the letters "H-E-L-P", not written with pen and ink, but with muddy paw-prints. She put the apple seeds in her pocket, and read the message again. A tear rolled down her cheek, as she ran toward the big building.

CHAPTER 14

Thank
You

THE NEXT days were filled with adventure for the hungry little family. It was Trasher who first discovered the gifts which brought his family safely through their period of near starvation. He had been scrounging for food near the wall, and to his surprise, found two more apples. Everyone agreed that Furry-Ball's letter had worked. The little Upright was responding to Furry-Ball's plea for help. She had understood. Every day they would return to find more food on the wall—sometimes fruit, sometimes bread, and once, something delicious, crisp and sweet.

Methuselah was very quick to remind them that it was undoubtedly The Maker prompting the little Upright to provide for them so generously.

"Do you think she knows The Maker?" asked Posie.

"I'm a-thinkin' she does, Little Flower," he admitted.

"Can we become friends, then?" she eagerly questioned.

"I'm a-feared it's already happened," he replied. "Of The Maker's doin' to be sure. His way of providin' for us when we right near starved to death. But iffen we're to be friends beyond that, He'll have to show us."

"But how, Grandfather?"

"Well, hasn't The Maker brought us this far without us a-hurtin' for shelter or food? Why, I've known The Maker for many a year and He's never been late in showin' me what to do. He's always on time. I'm jest not sure how He'll show us, but I'm sure He will, when we need to know. Meanwhile, Little One, you can jest be thankful for the Upright's friendship that's already come our way."

A sad expression came upon Posie's face. "Well, that's just it, Grandfather," answered Posie. "We haven't said 'thank you' at all except by giving her the gold band—and now we have nothing else to give her. We have only enough food to live on ourselves. If only we had something to give her."

Methuselah grew thoughtful. "Gifts ain't the only way to say 'thank you'—sometimes actin' kindly or speakin' a kind word is jest as good," he reminded.

"If only I could think of a kind thing to do for her—or if I knew how to speak her language, I'd say 'thank you,' Grandfather. But we don't have a white leaf to write on and I don't know their word for 'thank you.'"

"Well, it looks like either The Maker'll be givin' you a kind idea, or He'll provide a white leaf to write on. Meanwhile, jest in case, we'd better study up on the Code a bit—to be ready to say 'thank you' in Upright language, iffen The Maker provides."

No sooner had Methuselah spoken these words than Trasher arrived back from a scouting trip to the wall with cries of—"Food! And something else!"

Clambering over each other, the family quickly gathered around as he drew the mysterious objects from his yellow scarf. Tantalizing smells filled the air when he uncovered a whole pile of colorful, little, rock-like foods wrapped in a white leaf.

While the delicious smells had an almost magical hold on the other children, Posie saw something far more significant—the white leaf! Scooping up the crumpled paper in her paw, she carried it to a safe place in the hollow log. And, for the second time in her life, she whispered, "Thank you, Dear Maker!"

There was much discussion as to which of the colored rock-like foods was best. Trasher liked yellow best, while Puddly's choice was green. The ladies seemed to prefer red, and Seeker and Furry-Ball voted for purple. During all this chatter no one seemed to notice Methuselah's absence. It was only later that they realized he had been carefully studying the Code, and they brought him some of the food just as he was finishing his research.

"Try this, Grandfather," offered Puddly. "I think green tastes the best. By the way, what are you studying so hard?"

"Our next document, Son," replied Methuselah. He sampled a piece of the green rock food. "Tastes right fine, but the red looks mighty temptin' too!"

Handing him a red piece, Puddly asked, "What will the next document say, Grandfather?"

"The only thing we *can* say, Son—'Thank you!' The Maker knows we're thankful, but the little Upright needs to know too!"

There was an awkward silence because for a moment they were all ashamed that they had received so much and never before thought of thanking the giver. Then they all spoke at once with comments like, "You're right," and "How could we have forgotten?" and "Do you think it's too late?" Methuselah then told them of the plan. Meanwhile Posie ran to get the white leaf on which they could write their message.

As Trasher began to smooth out the paper, his eye caught a bright burst of colors on the other side.

"Look!" he exclaimed, "There's something on the back!" And, as he turned it over, they all crowded close to see what was on it.

No one could speak at first. The colors were so beautifully woven together that they looked almost lifelike. Furry-Ball instinctively reached out to touch it. Discovering it to be smooth and flat, his second reaction was one of disappointment. "It's not real," he said. (Of course, Furry-Ball had never seen a picture before.)

"No, it's like when you look in the water and see yourself," explained Trasher.

"But this is different," said Puddly. "It's not wet."

Soon a lively discussion went back and forth about the meaning of the picture. They all agreed that it was, in fact, a picture of an Upright family, but only one seemed to be in the "upright" position. There was disagreement as to what the others were doing. They were in a strange position. You couldn't call it standing, and they weren't sitting or lying down, and yet, the closed eyes made them think that perhaps this was the way Uprights slept. Some thought it had another meaning, however, and were sure the Upright symbols underneath would shed some light on the problem.

Dipping their paws in mud, they carefully copied the symbols on a stone for further study. Then, just as carefully, and after much practice, Posie wrote "Thank you" on the white side. Grandfather's research had been successful.

CHAPTER 15

A
Mystery

"I WONDER what it means," thought Puddly, looking at the curious marks they had copied from the white leaf.

It was several days later, when the weather was cold and nippy—much too cold for a food-gathering expedition—that the whole family gathered to watch Methuselah and Seeker translate the Upright symbols. Their own document had been delivered, and evidently received, because more treats had been left for them on the wall.

They were more determined than ever to discover what these symbols meant. Trasher thought that perhaps these were the names of the various Uprights in the picture— definitely not *their* Uprights, at least none whom they had ever seen. Seeker felt it was not a message from their little Upright either because, while certain symbols looked the same, they were differently formed, not at all the way she wrote. Fairly bursting with curiosity, they had great difficulty restraining themselves from interfering with Methuselah's work. Each tried to find some "busy" work to do, but all managed somehow to be working as close to Methuselah and Seeker as possible. Posie had gotten the closest. She was dusting right around Methuselah's paws, concentrating more on what Methuselah was doing than on her dusting job. Puddly and Furry-Ball added their dusting services, each trying to get closer to Methuselah, until one of them dusted his paw by mistake.

"It ain't gonna hasten things up a bit, young-uns," an irritated Methuselah warned, after being dusted. "But to satisfy your curiosity a bit, I'll tell you the results of my studyin' so far."

"Have you finished?" queried Furry-Ball.

"Not entirely, Furry-Boy," answered Methuselah. "But I've completed a good piece of it."

"Well, what does it say, Grandfather?" an eager Furry-Ball continued.

"It says, 'Let us kneel before . . .'" replied Methuselah.

"What does 'kneel' mean? And 'before' *whom,* Grandfather?" demanded Posie.

"That remains to be seen, Little Flower. And the sooner your father and I can work in peace and quiet, the sooner we'll solve the mystery."

The two then set about to unravel the meaning of the mystery, while the "younger set" gathered in a huddle to attempt to put the pieces of the puzzle together themselves.

"What does it all mean, Trash?" asked Posie.

"Remember the group of Uprights in the picture?" he reminded them. "I think the 'us' is them. And that strange position they're in must be called kneeling. Remember how they were all in that position except for one standing in front of them?"

"But why are they doing that?" an impatient Furry-Ball asked.

Trasher

"To show that the one standing is more important than they are," answered Trasher, "but Grandfather probably knows for sure."

"And who is that one upright who is not kneeling?" quizzed Posie.

A perplexed group of young raccoons went round and round in conversational circles, while a dedicated group of older, scholarly raccoons painstakingly studied symbol by symbol until the solution was found.

Once again, the entire family crowded around Methuselah and Seeker with hushed anticipation as they awaited the solution to their mysterious puzzle.

Methuselah and Seeker did not seem in any hurry to share their findings, but finally Methuselah began slowly. "I think the Uprights kneel before someone they love or respect, maybe even worship. It looks mighty like we've discovered the name of the Upright that them other Uprights are a-kneelin' before."

"Well, who?" an impatient Posie begged.

"His name's 'The Lord,' " said Methuselah quietly.

"Who's that?" asked Puddly. "We don't know anyone by that name."

"Is that all it said?" asked Posie, disappointment in her voice.

"No," responded Methuselah, and he hesitated. "The whole document reads, 'Let us kneel before the Lord (at this point he paused), our Maker.' "

"The Lord, our Maker!" they all exclaimed in shocked disbelief. For a while, no one spoke.

Finally, Posie asked incredulously, "Grandfather, is it true—is The Maker an Upright?"

"I don't rightly understand it, Little Flower, but 'twould appear so. However, we'll have to do some more studyin' before we can 'cept it as true. It jest don't make sense after them Uprights turned against Him—for Him to turn around and be one of them," responded Methuselah.

Silence set in—the kind of silence that comes when something very shocking has just been said. And for this family, something shocking had been said. The Maker had become an Upright.

After a long pause, Furry-Ball spoke up. "I wonder why He didn't come as a raccoon?"

"I've often wondered 'bout that m'self," answered Methuselah.

"Well, it proves one thing, Grandfather," said Posie assuredly. "It proves that our Upright knows about The Maker! I just knew she did!"

"That it does, Little Flower, that it does!"

Let us kneel before the Lord Our Maker

CHAPTER 16

*A*way
in a
Manger

COLD WIND bit through Posie's fur, but on this day she didn't care. Trasher, Puddly and Furry-Ball had joined her on a secret mission—to find more documents to translate. It wasn't really a secret mission, but they were trying to make it so. Trasher, as usual, led the way, his yellow scarf trailing behind him. Trasher saw himself as a military leader in command of troops, and it seemed natural and fitting that he should "take charge." The others followed him gladly, since he usually could be counted upon to do the right thing.

"Do you think The Maker really came as an Upright?" Posie thought out loud.

"It's beginning to look that way," responded Trasher. "But we need more proof. If only we could find more documents—then we would know for sure."

"But, *why* would He do that, Trash?" Then Posie answered her own question. "I guess if He came as an Upright, that means He must *really* love them. And if they were all like our Upright, I can understand why He does." Posie's perplexed look changed to a softer expression. "I'm glad Grandfather let us go near the big house today," she sighed. "I think he's changing his mind about Uprights, don't you?"

"He might be," agreed Trasher, "but we still must be careful. We can't be sure that *all* Uprights are good."

They moved quickly until they reached the familiar wall. Then, sheltered from the biting wind, they stopped and waited for orders from their leader.

"Let's look for some documents around the back," said Trasher. "Waddler once told me that he often saw white leaves there in a big silver thing like a treasure chest. But first, you'd better all stay here while I take a quick look around the big house to make sure there are no Uprights. Don't move until I get back."

True to their word, they remained motionless, watching as Trasher disappeared behind the building. Before long he returned, described in detail what he saw, and outlined their next move.

"Posie, you and Furry-Ball keep close to the big house as you look for white leaves—stay behind the bushes as much as possible. Puddly, you go around the back. I saw a big silver thing that I think is full of white leaves. It looks just like the silver treasure chest Waddler described. See if you can look inside. Meanwhile, I'll circle around the big house in case an Upright comes. If I spot one, I'll signal. Okay, everyone to his position," ordered Trasher, "and above all, keep quiet."

Carefully, and very quietly, they all "headed off" to do their jobs. Posie and Furry-Ball kept close to the building, hiding behind bushes whenever possible. Trasher made a large circle, following the tree line to better conceal himself.

Only Puddly was visible as he climbed up the slippery side of a large metal object. Though you or I might have seen only a garbage can, Puddly recognized it at once to be the treasure chest that Trasher had described, and thought it was simply lovely as it shone in the sunlight. Peeking inside, his eyes widened. "It's full of white leaves!" he shouted excitedly.

Nearly overcome with curiosity, Posie motioned for him to go down into the chest and bring up some leaves. He did so at once, but could not keep quiet.

"Wait 'til you see this!" he yelled. "Here's a picture of a baby Upright, and he's sleeping on pine needles just like us!" He threw the picture over the edge, and dove back into the garbage can to find more.

Posie was just about to race over and retrieve the picture when several things happened at once. Out of the corner of her eye, she saw Furry-Ball busily investigating a back door that had been left open just a crack. They were both completely unprepared for what happened next. The door came flying open and out stepped an Upright—one whom they had never seen before. He was carrying a big brown bag and thankfully did not look down, or he would have seen a little raccoon trembling with fear. To avoid being seen, or worse yet stepped on, Furry-Ball did the only safe

thing he could—he scurried quickly inside the door, not realizing that it would slam shut. But Posie did not see this. She was so startled by the Upright's sudden appearance that she made a wild dash for safety, ducked under a low branch and stayed as still as she could.

Meanwhile, Puddly got no warning at all for what happened next. One minute he was gathering white leaves, burrowing deep into the pile, and the next he thought he was being buried alive from above, as the Upright dumped the brown bag filled with white leaves down on top of him. No one dared to move for what seemed an awfully long time. At last Trasher emerged from behind a tree and ran quickly toward the silver object.

"It's safe—he's gone!" he yelled, motioning at the same time for Posie to help him dig Puddly out.

"Hurry!" came a muffled voice from inside the silver container. "I can't breathe!" It was clear Puddly was beginning to panic. Posie and Trasher worked feverishly to free him. When at last Puddly's face poked through they all heaved a sigh of relief.

With that task completed, Posie looked around anxiously for her little brother. "I don't see Furry-Ball anywhere!" she cried.

"Furry-Ball is inside the big house, and the door is shut!" Trasher shouted. "I saw it!"

The two younger raccoons, in a state of shock, were unable to move as Trasher ran to the door and clawed it frantically. But eventually they came to their senses and joined Trasher, working until they were exhausted.

"It's no use, Trash," sighed Puddly. A pitiful whine came from inside.

"Furry-Ball . . . Furry-Ball . . . is that you?" shouted Trasher anxiously.

Puddly

"Am I going to have to stay here forever, Trash?" Furry-Ball's worried little voice asked.

"No, Furry-Ball. Now listen carefully. We'll get you out, but you have to help us. First, go around to all the clear stone openings and see if you can get any of them open. We'll follow you around the outside."

Window after window was tried on the inside by Furry-Ball and on the outside by the others, but to no avail. None would open. It was getting dark, and they all realized how hungry they were.

Furry-Ball put his feelings into words. "I'm so tired and hungry—I wish I could just go home and eat supper and go to bed."

"But you can't right now," said Posie gently, "because we can't find a way to get you out."

"How long will it take?" pled Furry-Ball. "I might starve."

Trasher made several suggestions at this point. "First, someone needs to go home and tell them all what's happened. Maybe they'll come and help. Second, Furry-Ball needs to find a good safe place to hide, in case the Uprights come back. He could take a nap while one of us goes home."

"But you won't leave me alone, will you?" begged Furry-Ball, trembling.

"No, Furry-Ball, we'll stay right here. But look all over for a good hiding place—then come back and tell us where it is, okay?"

Furry-Ball did as he was told while the others decided who should go home. Trasher thought it best that Puddly go since it was dark and there was the possibility of meeting their enemies. He gave him his yellow scarf filled with the white leaves they had gathered from the silver container.

It was then that Posie remembered the picture that

Puddly had thrown over the edge before the big Upright had come. "Wait—there's one more," she said picking up the discarded paper. She stared at the picture in amazement. The others crowded around and for a minute they became so absorbed in the picture that they forgot all about Furry-Ball.

"Just like you said, Puddly," exclaimed Posie. "A baby Upright sleeping on pine needles."

Furry-Ball's shouts jarred them back to reality. "I think I found just the right spot. There's a whole different part to this house—to get there you have to go up," he said.

"Couldn't you find a spot down in this part so we can see you?" asked Trasher.

"No," answered Furry-Ball. "Everything's too smooth and hard, or else it's too open and not safe enough. But up in the other part there's a good place to hide."

"Describe it to us," responded Trasher.

"Well, at first I thought I had run into more Uprights. From far back it sure looked like them, but they didn't move, so I went closer. Sure enough, they weren't alive at all—in fact, they didn't even smell—they just looked alive. But when I touched them, they were cold and smooth. They didn't move, so I went up real close. They were all gathered around a strange piece of furniture that had dried grass in it. It looked an awful lot like the picture you told us about, Puddly. There was a baby Upright sleeping on the dried grass but he wasn't real either. Since the baby isn't really alive, I think it would make a real good place for me to sleep too—I could cover myself with that dried grass. And it look's so soft! Please let me hide there—but promise not to go away?" he begged.

"It sure sounds just like what we see in this picture," Puddly said, putting their thoughts into words, "and it does sound like a safe place. What do you think, Trash?"

"As long as he's sure those Uprights aren't alive and not just sleeping," answered Trasher. He turned toward Furry-Ball still waiting patiently on the other side of the window. "But first, give one of those Uprights a little nip, in case he's really alive, but don't bite him hard. And then get ready to run if he moves. If he doesn't, it's safe. And don't sleep long, take only a little nap." They waved to one another, and then Furry-Ball disappeared.

It seemed like ages before Puddly returned with Seeker. Aunt Serenity had packed some food for them in Trasher's yellow scarf, and they ate hungrily. While they were eating, Seeker began an examination of the windows. In the course of his investigation, he discovered a little object that he felt sure held the secret to opening them. He called for Furry-Ball to grab hold and turn it, but no answer came after calling for a long time.

"Furry-Ball . . . Furry! Oh, why won't he answer!" Posie joined in. Still Furry-Ball did not come. Finally, when they had waited an awfully long time, they agreed to take turns guarding while the others slept. As each took his turn, and still Furry-Ball did not wake up, concern grew for his safety.

Darkness had fallen by the time it was Posie's turn, but her alert eyes caught the movement—two Uprights were coming toward the building. As they came closer, she recognized familiar faces and almost said aloud, "Thank goodness they're ours." They went up the steps and into the building. "But Furry-Ball's in there!" she had almost forgotten. Jumping up, she raced to where the others were sleeping, and gave them the news.

Seeker wasted no time in giving orders and explaining their tasks. "Each of you hide by one of the clear stone openings and tell Furry-Ball what to turn in case he comes. We'll just have to hope for the best," he added.

They responded instantly and none too soon, for toward the steps came a long line of Uprights, one by one disappearing into the building.

"Oh, poor Furry-Ball," said Posie anxiously. "Where is he—why doesn't he come?" Suddenly strange sounds distracted her thoughts. They came from far above her. She had heard those same sounds before, but this time, added to them were strange new sounds. "Could these strange sounds be from the Uprights?" she wondered.

Furry-Ball, who was up above, also heard those strange new sounds and instinctively poked his head out of the dried grass. A shocked expression came over his face as he looked out at a room filled with Uprights, standing and making a lovely noise together. Since they were not looking directly at him, he thought that perhaps, if he stayed very still, they might think *he* was the baby Upright. So, he tried his best to look like a baby Upright. (What Furry-Ball did not realize was that baby Uprights just do not have bushy tails and masks.) Now he might have succeeded in this deception had it not been for a little Upright in the front row who had been looking at the life-sized crèche.

"A raccoon in the manger!" he yelled.

Shouts of indignation brought Furry-Ball quickly to his senses. He jumped out of the manger, dashed straight down the aisle, down the stairs, and into one of the rooms. Above him was one of the clear stone openings and on the other side was Posie, motioning frantically to him to turn the little object on his side. Several big Uprights ran past the open door, completely missing him. He was so distraught that he could not even follow Posie's directions. Instead, he screamed desperately, "Help!"

And help came, but not from Posie. Furry-Ball saw a little hand reach right past him, turn the little knob and lift the window upward. A feeling of relief engulfed him as he

"A raccoon in the manger!" he yelled.

saw once again the familiar face of their little Upright. He dashed through the opening, but once on the other side, he and Posie simultaneously turned for one more look. Their friend was waving. Gratitude filled their hearts and they waved back.

Joined by the others, they raced homeward, not knowing whether they felt more relieved or excited about the events of the evening. But in their wildest dreams they could not have imagined that they had experienced their very first Christmas.

CHAPTER 17

An Enemy
Becomes a Friend

I T WAS true. The Maker had come as an Upright! Their research had proven beyond any doubt that He had come as a tiny baby.

"If only I hadn't pushed him out of the way," sighed Furry-Ball when he realized who it was in that manger alongside of him. "But I was so sure He wasn't alive—He didn't move at all and He was so cold!" he added, trying to justify his actions.

They were all confused, but tended to agree with Seeker's conclusion—that this was not The Maker—but another of the Upright's "pictures" of what The Maker looked like. In fact, they were sure that by now He must be fully grown—like the original picture they had seen.

More pieces of evidence were put together every day as Trasher and Puddly made additional trips to the silver treasure chest.

"Why would He come as an Upright?" The question burned within their hearts. "And where does He live?" was still another concern.

The answer to that question came one day when they translated a new document that Trasher had found. It filled them with sorrow when they read, "Foxes have holes and birds of the air have nests, but the Son of Man has no place to lay His head." They knew by now that this referred to none other than The Maker, and they were amazed that He would be treated this way.

"To think that the Uprights would not even share their homes," said Posie indignantly.

"Then why don't we?" suggested Furry-Ball. And he meant it.

"That's a right good idea, Son, iffen we could find Him," Methuselah agreed.

"Maybe He visits them in the big house sometimes," added Puddly, "even though they don't share their homes with Him."

More discussion followed—some not too flattering to Uprights, I'm afraid, and for this reason we won't mention it. But the conclusion to their discussion was that they would all make a concerted effort to find The Maker, and once they did, offer Him their hospitality.

With this in mind, they began to make major improvements to their home. Tidy-Paw cleaned with a new zeal every day, reminding them of the possibility of a "Guest." It was she who thought of using a piece of "clear stone" they had found to cover an opening near the door. (Actually it was somewhat softer than stone, but clear nonetheless.) Seeker and Trasher wedged it into the opening in such a way that there was hardly a crack. They all remarked about how cozy it made their home and how much more light it let in. Without the wind, they were so much warmer, and translating became much easier with the extra light. They were sure The Maker would be very comfortable with this new improvement.

And then one day while translating a document, they heard it—the loud crunching sound of footsteps.

"Could it be Him?" they asked in unison. They were

afraid to look outside, and only when the noise had disappeared did they gather courage to peek out. There at the bottom of the tree lay a bundle of food. They scrambled down to examine it.

"I'd say it was from our little Upright," announced Trasher. "This is just like the food she's left for us before. And these footprints are about her size. But, just to be safe, how about Puddly and I following them to make sure."

They left hurriedly, but Puddly was back in only minutes. He barged through the doorway, and panting heavily, gasped, "Come quick! Waddler's dying—he's caught in a trap—Trasher's with him!"

Posie raced after the disappearing shapes of Puddly, Seeker and Furry-Ball. "Wait for me!" she called until she finally caught up. Puddly, in between breaths, blurted out the story.

"It was our Upright, all right. We followed her tracks all the way to the brook and saw her crossing there. She headed toward the big house. We were just about to turn around, when we noticed some more tracks. They weren't hers, but we decided to follow them anyway. They went along the brook for quite a while. We didn't see any Uprights, but then we saw him—poor Waddler. It was terrible—oh, I hope he doesn't die!"

No one spoke for the rest of the trip until they reached the clearing. Then Seeker took charge.

"Puddly, you come with me and help. Furry-Ball and Posie, go back by that big clump of trees, then climb up and watch. If an Upright comes, warn us." Posie and Furry-Ball scrambled up a tree to watch.

As Puddly and Seeker approached Waddler, they heard his pathetic cries. A combination of sympathy and anger welled up in Puddly as he and Seeker surveyed the situation. There was Waddler, held fast by the trap, while Trasher worked feverishly to free him. Adding their strength to Trasher's the raccoons attempted to pry open the trap. It had closed on Waddler's tail, and though he had lost much blood, there was hope that he could be saved if only they could open the trap. But try as they would, the trap would not open and Waddler's cries continued. Seeker then thought of another idea. Perhaps wedging a stick through the trap's mouth would work. Using all their strength as leverage, they felt the trap beginning to open, when sud-

denly the stick snapped, and they found themselves in a heap holding the broken end.

Not willing to give up, Trasher shouted his idea. "A rock! It has to be sharp, though. A rock can't break! Puddly, you stay with Waddler." He and Seeker headed off to find the right rock.

"Oh, Waddler, I'm so sorry for you," said Puddly as a tear slipped down his furry cheek. "Don't give up—it won't be long now and you'll be free."

Puddly's words were interrupted at that point by Posie's warning yell, "An Upright!"

Panic gripped Puddly's heart and he felt torn between staying to defend Waddler or running to meet the enemy before he got to Waddler. Suddenly, he knew what he must do. With new courage, he said, "I'll try and head him off, Waddler. Trash and Father will be back soon and get you out."

Numb with fear, Puddly stumbled toward the Upright, not knowing just what he would do to stop him. As he passed by the tree where Posie and Furry-Ball were hiding, he heard Posie's quiet little voice.

"Oh, Maker, please help Puddly."

Almost immediately, two things happened. Puddly came face to face with the Upright, and an idea popped into his mind as to what he should do. The Upright was, as he had thought, a stranger. This one had short hair and a down-turned mouth, and no doubt was the one responsible for Waddler's sad plight. But the most terrifying thing of all was his weapon—a huge stick.

Puddly quickly put his idea into action. He assumed the guise of a crippled raccoon and hobbled away from Waddler's direction. Just as he guessed, the Upright followed him, probably thinking he had an easy prey. At times, Puddly let the Upright get dangerously close, so that he would not give up and return to Waddler. Farther and farther he led him, hoping to buy time for Seeker and Trasher to free Waddler. Several times he saw the stick swing toward his back, and Puddly shuddered at the thought of what it could do to him. But he put the thought out of his mind and concentrated on diverting the Upright's attention from Waddler.

Meanwhile, Seeker and Trasher had returned with a sharp rock, only to find Puddly gone.

"Help Puddly!" cried Waddler, in a voice barely audible.

"Puddly's heading off the Upright!" yelled Posie, frantically.

Seeker dropped the rock near Waddler and he and Trasher ran to Puddly's rescue. Following their tracks, they soon came upon the two. One look at Puddly hobbling slowly convinced them that the Upright had crippled him. Seeker and Trasher crept quietly up behind the Upright. They were filled with anger, and in unison, snarled as loudly as they could, catching the Upright by surprise. Turning, he dropped his stick, took one look at the two angry faces, and ran off in the direction of the big house.

"Am I glad you came," breathed Puddly with a sigh of relief. Recovering miraculously from his crippled state, he shouted, "We've got to get back and save Waddler!"

"You're okay?" questioned Seeker. "We thought the Upright had wounded you."

"I just did that to trick him—to lure him away from Waddler," answered Puddly.

"Good thinking," replied Seeker as they headed back to the clearing.

To their complete surprise, Waddler was gone, except for one part of him. There lying in the trap was his beautiful tail—his pride and joy.

Posie's voice soon answered their questions. "He's over here—come quickly!"

They hurried over to her hiding place and found her bending over Waddler. "Trash, let me have your scarf," she cried. "I think we can use it to stop the bleeding." Trasher handed it to her quickly and she wound it tightly around the remainder of Waddler's tail.

He smiled weakly. "I'm free," he whispered, and closed his eyes.

"Oh, don't die, Waddler," begged Puddly. Another tear slipped down his cheek.

"We've got to get him home somehow," said a determined Seeker. "Furry-Ball, you run ahead and tell the others what's happened. And tell them to get some food and water ready. He's very weak. We don't have time to make a stretcher, so the rest of you help me, and together we'll *be* a stretcher."

Carefully they lifted Waddler's helpless body onto their backs and slowly made their way home. On the way, Posie described in detail how it was that Waddler freed himself.

"Before Furry-Ball and I could get to him, he wedged the rock in the trap all by himself. The trap was just opening when all of a sudden, he lost his strength and the trap snapped back." Posie choked back a sob at this point. "It was awful—I'm so glad Furry-Ball didn't see it happen. It must have hurt so. But at least he's free." Some tears trickled down her cheeks.

Trasher spoke up. "Posie, you run ahead and help get ready—we can carry him without you." He took over her position and she obeyed, relieved to be away from all her painful memories of the last hour.

It wasn't long before they were safely home. Tidy-Paw and Aunt Serenity took over at this point, making Waddler comfortable and most important, getting food and water into his weakened body. Then, they all waited, and watched over their wounded guest. After what seemed an endless amount of time, their vigil was rewarded. Waddler opened his eyes and whispered again, "I'm free!"

It was Puddly this time who joined Posie in a quiet, "Thank you, Dear Maker."

CHAPTER 18

A
Celebration

THERE was no doubt about it! Day by day, Waddler *was* getting better. Aunt Serenity and Tidy-Paw kept the family busy bringing water in an empty shell Trasher had found by the brook. Waddler drank endlessly at first, but soon the day came when he asked for solid food.

"The Maker be praised!" exclaimed Methuselah. "Waddler's on the mend. It's The Maker's doin' of course!"

"That's it!" announced Posie. "That's the reason why The Maker came!"

Everyone looked with startled expressions that seemed to say, "What do you mean, 'the reason He came'?"

Posie explained. "Don't you remember the leaf that we translated just the other day?" Their furrowed brows showed that they still did not follow her reasoning. She began again. "Waddler's tail is almost healed," she said. "And though we brought him water and made him comfortable, none of *us* healed him. Grandfather's right—it's all from The Maker! It's just like the picture we saw. And remember the words we translated? The Upright said to The Maker, 'Once I was blind, but now I see'? Maybe that's what The Maker came to do—to heal those Uprights when they get sick—just like He did for Waddler."

"'Tis a mighty good reason, Little Flower, for The Maker to come," agreed Methuselah. "There's been a heap of sickness both to them Uprights and the likes of us, and knowin' Him, He cares about each one. Why, Old Uncle Seth used to say He even knew when a sparrow fell. But I'd be surprised iffen that was the *only* reason He came."

"Why, Grandfather?" asked Posie.

"It'd take more than healing their sick bodies to make them return to The Maker," he explained. "He'd have to heal their hearts too."

"How could He do that, Grandfather?" asked Furry-Ball.

"I'm a-wishin' I knew, Son," he said softly.

Their conversation was interrupted at that moment by the sound of familiar footsteps coming from down below. And, to their delight, another big leaf filled with delicious goodies was left for them to enjoy. Knowing that it was a gift from their little Upright, they felt no concern that their hidden home had been discovered. They offered Waddler his choice of food, but for a long time he didn't take any, nor did he speak. He just stared off into space. When finally he chose a piece of food, he said, "Why are you all so kind to me? You should hate me! Do you remember when your food was stolen? I was the one who told them where your supply was."

Methuselah spoke up. "We don't hate you, Son. And we don't hate them neither. You see, The Maker made us all. And we still follow Him. That's why we live at peace with them. And we've always kind of felt that you really wasn't one of them—you was jest a-followin' them so's you could belong."

"You're right. I never really belonged, though. And

what's more, they got me to do lots of bad things—things I really knew were wrong."

"Iffen you was uncomfortable doin' wrong, maybe The Maker's callin' you away from them, Son," suggested Methuselah.

"Yes, I believe He is—but where can I go?" asked Waddler with a little catch in his voice.

"Why not stay with us?" they all said in unison.

"You mean I could stay?" he asked incredulously. "I don't have to go back?"

"'Course not, Son," answered Methuselah. "You're as welcome as any of us. And I think The Maker'd be mighty pleased too if you'd join us."

"Do you really think so, Grandfather?" and then he corrected himself. "Oh, I'm sorry—but could I call you 'Grandfather'?"

"I'd be right proud iffen you'd call me 'Grandfather,' Son," replied Methuselah.

"Thank you, Grandfather." A big smile spread across his face. "Oh, it'll be so good to have a real family again. You see, I've been so lonely ever since . . . ever since . . ." and then Waddler stopped and looked away sadly.

"Ever since what?" asked Puddly sympathetically.

"Ever since I was separated from my first family," he responded. "It was a long time ago," he went on, "and in a different country—the one beyond the big house."

The family of raccoons leaned forward with interest as Waddler told his story. They had heard once or twice of this different country, but had never been there.

Waddler told how their country had become filled more and more with Uprights until their food supply was dangerously low. Some of his neighbors had begun to fight back by raiding Upright gardens, but not Waddler's family.

They had decided to look for a new country. After a long journey, the family had found just the spot—plenty of food and no Uprights, or so they thought. And then, one day, after returning home from a food-gathering trip, Waddler had seen a huge monster made by Uprights, knocking down trees with one blow and digging up the forest where their home had been. But worst of all, his family was gone and he had never found them again. It was while searching for them that he had run into Needlenose and Rabid and had joined their band of night raiders. But always he had secretly hoped to find his own family again.

"We'll help you in your search, Waddler," Trasher encouraged him. "But meanwhile, just allow *us* to be your family."

Aunt Serenity broke the somber mood. "It's not every day The Maker sends us a new member! I'd say this calls for a celebration!"

An explosion of activity accompanied the children's shouts of joy. Tidy-Paw and Aunt Serenity began to prepare food while Posie and Furry-Ball looked for decorations. They decided to use some of the brightly colored leaves Puddly had brought home from the silver container. Posie hung the high pictures while Furry-Ball hung the low, and then they both stood back to admire their finished work.

"Oh, it's beautiful, Furry-Ball, but if only we had flowers," she sighed.

"We could use pine cones and berries instead," suggested Furry-Ball. Posie agreed excitedly, and off they went in search of decorations for the table.

Trasher and Puddly talked quietly as they planned games for the celebration. Meanwhile, Methuselah and Seeker prepared a special bed of pine needles and dry leaves near the table for Waddler.

And Waddler, from his window, took in all these preparations. His heart seemed about to burst with sheer excitement. "I belong," he thought happily, "I really belong!"

After what seemed only minutes to those making preparations, and hours to Waddler who watched, the time came to start the celebration. Gently, they carried Waddler to his place of honor by the table. Bright berries, arranged with greens and pine cones decorated each place, and delicious scents of food filled the air. The family's radiant smiles expressed an unvoiced "Welcome!" and Waddler's tear-filled eyes answered back, "Thank you!"

Then the meal began. It seemed as if Waddler had always been a part of the family. Conversation flowed easily, punctuated by laughter and joking. Compliments were given for the tasty food and festive decorations, and then it was time for the games to start.

Though Waddler couldn't take part, he howled with laughter as Furry-Ball, trying to clear Seeker's back in leapfrog, landed on top of him, tried to hang on, and then slid unceremoniously down his nose. Next came a swinging contest. A long vine had been hung from an overhanging branch. Puddly was having so much fun swinging that he didn't even mind when Trasher beat him in distance. Posie was the winner of the "guess what it is" game. They had to close their eyes and Posie wanted desperately to peek, but she won fairly by carefully running her little fingers over each object.

Puddly

And then Puddly brought out his secret treasure. The whole family gazed in admiration at the smooth stone ball he had found while digging for food. Its blue and white colors suggested a sky filled with soft fluffy clouds. It seemed wrong to use such an object of beauty for a game, but soon Posie joined the others in rolling the ball toward a stick. One by one, the competitors were narrowed down until only Seeker and Methuselah were left. All eyes were fastened on the two as the last round began.

Suddenly, a loud, nasty, but familiar cackle came from outside the clearing, breaking their festive mood. Spinning around, they found themselves face to face with Needlenose, Rabid, Slinky and Raider. They froze with fear as Needlenose began his taunts.

"So you lost your tail, eh Waddler?" He cackled again.

As a protective measure, the family encircled Waddler. But while he couldn't defend himself in body, a new courage filled his soul. Looking Needlenose straight in the eye, he said, "Yes, I lost a tail, but I gained a family."

"So you think they're your friends?" challenged Raider.

"They didn't leave me to die like you did—they saved my life," he answered.

"Oh, come on now, Waddler—you know you'll miss all the excitement on this side," reasoned Needlenose.

"If you mean the excitement of being caught in a trap— no, I won't miss that," he assured them.

Rabid

"Oh, I get it," answered Slinky, "you're mad at us just because of a little accident. You know it wasn't our fault. Why not be friends again and come back to our side?"

"It wasn't an accident," responded Waddler. "I should never have been there in the first place. And you're right—it wasn't your fault—it was mine for listening to you. But I want you to know that I am still your friend, even though I don't plan on going back to your side. You see, I've decided to follow The Maker and I can do it best by staying with this family."

Loud cackles from all four followed. "Well, when you get tired of following The Maker," said Needlenose sarcastically, "just come on back where you belong." Then as suddenly as they had come, they were gone.

After a few moments of silence, Waddler spoke. "They don't realize that *this* is where I belong."

"That you do, Son," answered Methuselah.

CHAPTER 19

Clues

SPRING was in the air! Oh, there were still patches of snow here and there, but the air was warm and filled with the scent of things coming to life again. Tidy-Paw had pronounced Waddler well enough to go out for a walk, and so Posie, Puddly and Trasher had volunteered to accompany him. Furry-Ball tagged along close behind as usual.

"You sure look funny without your tail, Waddler," said Furry-Ball with an honesty so typical of little raccoons.

"Furry-Ball, that's not at all kind," scolded Posie. "And now you've hurt Waddler's feelings."

"That's okay," said Waddler, "I guess I'm so thankful to be alive that I don't even miss my tail. There was a time when I felt very proud of it—but now I feel prouder to be a part of this family, even without my tail."

"I think I know what you mean," added Puddly. "And it's funny, but I've gotten so used to seeing you without your tail that I don't even notice that you're different from us . . . I guess because you really aren't, inside, that is."

"I'm sorry I said you look funny, Waddler." Furry-Ball had been thinking that his comment, although honest, wasn't very kind. He tried to make up for it. "If there were a way I could give you *my* tail, I would."

"Thank you," replied Waddler. "That's very kind. But you know, for the first time in my life, I don't really feel that I need one. You might say it was losing my tail that gave me my freedom!"

They walked on. It was fun to show their new friend all their favorite spots—the best hiding places, the place where Puddly had dug up the smooth, round ball he treasured, and the places where Posie found her best flowers for her daily wreath.

In fact, while the others were digging near Puddly's spot in hopes of finding another ball, Posie had found a new treasure. "Will someone come and help me?" she called. "I've found the most beautiful things! They're not really flowers, and they're so soft . . . almost like fur!" Somehow, her old wreaths didn't seem to compare to the beauty she could now picture in a wreath made of fur.

(Of course, it wasn't really fur. But, never having seen or felt Pussy-Willow buds before, it was like fur to her.) She reached up as high as she could, and in reaching, her paw grazed a sharp bramble bush.

"Ouch!" she whimpered. "Watch out for those sharp things, Trash."

Trasher carefully avoided the bramble bush as he bent the branches down to Posie. Breaking off the most beautiful ones, she wasted no time in weaving them into a new wreath. "How special," she thought excitedly to herself, "a fur wreath!"

As they walked along, Posie kept working, using her forepaws to weave, while waddling along on her two hind legs. Gradually a circle took shape. Looking up momentarily, she realized they had already come to the brook.

"Let's sit down and rest a while," she suggested, thinking of how tired Waddler must be. They did, and Posie took advantage of the time to put the finishing touches on her wreath. She tried it on, and, finding a quiet little pool of water at the edge, she looked at her reflection. How beautiful it looked, and how soft it felt.

"It matches my own fur!" she thought. And for the first time, she was glad she had fur instead of smooth skin like the Uprights. It was by far the loveliest wreath she had ever worn. She was enjoying herself immensely when her thoughts were abruptly interrupted.

"Hide!" yelled Trasher.

They dashed for cover and then peeked out to see what Trasher had seen. Fear gripped their hearts as they all saw him at once—the Upright who had tried to trap Waddler. And then as their eyes focused more clearly, their fear turned to horror and indignation.

Furry-Ball put it into words. "Look at his hat!" he cried. "That's Waddler's tail on his hat!" Furry-Ball choked back a sob. "And he's carrying one of those death traps!"

Tears filled their eyes as they watched the Upright slowly make his way along the edge of the brook. He seemed to be looking for something. Soon he was out of sight.

"He's trying to find our tracks," deduced Trasher. "Then he'll set the trap."

"I hate him," sobbed Furry-Ball. "He's not like our Upright—he's mean. And I'll bet he doesn't even know about The Maker."

"That's right, Furry-Ball, he doesn't," admitted Waddler.

"But how do you know, Waddler?" asked Posie. "Puddly and Trasher saw his tracks next to our little Upright's, so he must know her. And if she knows The Maker, she must have told him. Don't you see?"

"Well, you'd think she'd tell him, but maybe not," he answered.

Posie was quiet for a moment. "That can't be," she reasoned. "He probably didn't listen to her, or maybe he only knows The Maker a little. He probably doesn't realize The Maker loves us too."

"The reason I believe he doesn't know The Maker is that he never goes into the big house," responded Waddler. "I've watched many times and he never goes in. There's a difference between those who go in and those who don't."

"Do you really think so, Waddler?" Posie was extremely interested. "You seem to know so much about them. Tell us more about what you've seen!"

"Well, I *have* seen them quite a bit," he answered. "You see, they go in every seven days. Never him, though. But it doesn't surprise me about all the kind things your little Upright does for you—she *always* goes in. I love to watch them come out. They're so happy!"

Tidy-Paw

"How can you tell?" asked Posie.

"By their mouths," he replied. "They turn up a little bit and that means they're happy."

Posie and Furry-Ball exchanged knowing glances at each other. This confirmed what they believed.

"It's getting late," Trasher broke in. "We'd better get back home or they'll be worried about us." He started off and the others quickly followed.

It was almost meal-time when they got home. Aunt Serenity and Tidy-Paw had lunch waiting.

"One at a time!" Tidy-Paw had to remind them, as reports of the morning's events were shared. The older members hardly talked—they sat quietly and listened, sometimes asking a polite question or two, or adding an 'Oh my!' now and then. That is—all but Methuselah—he was absolutely quiet.

This was unusual for him, and when finally Posie noticed it, she asked politely, "Grandfather, what did you do this morning?"

"Why, I translated an important document, Little Flower."

"Oh, why didn't you tell us, Grandfather?" she asked.

"I'd 'a been happy to, iffen I'd been able to get a word in edgewise, My Dear," he answered. "I think I've found the clue we've been looking for."

Recovering from her embarrassment, curiosity got the better of her. "What did the document say, Grandfather?"

"It told the reason The Maker came—that's all."

Trasher carefully avoided the bramble bush
as he bent the branches down to Posie.

"Well, why, Grandfather, why did He come? *Please* tell us!" Her words reflected her impatience.

"It said that He came simply, 'to seek and to save that which was lost,' Little Flower."

And then the former method of conversation resumed—everyone talking at once with comments like, "'Lost' means the Uprights, of course" and "Do you think He's found them?" and "How can He save them?"

When the discussion ended, Methuselah voiced his conclusion. "We can't be sure iffen He's found 'em, but find 'em He will. And as to savin' them, He'll find a way to do it, of that you *can* be sure."

"That's what *I* need to do," stated Waddler.

Everyone looked at him in surprise.

"I'm going to try and find my family," he said.

"Don't you like our family, Waddler?" asked Furry-Ball, bewildered.

"Oh, yes, I do," he assured him. "That's why I want to find them. I'd like to invite them to come and live here too if that's all right with you."

"Do you think they'd want to follow The Maker's ways like we do?" questioned Posie.

"I think they would," he answered. "You see, they already know about Him—they just don't know *how* to follow Him."

"That's a mighty risky undertakin', Son," cautioned Methuselah.

"I know, Grandfather," he responded, "but I feel I owe this to them. They may not come, but at least they should have the chance."

"But what if you can't find them?" Trasher considered. "And if you did and they wouldn't come, would you stay there, or come back?"

Waddler

"I'd come back. But, last night an idea came to me—one that I never thought of before," answered Waddler. "I think they might have gone back to our first home. And, you see, I never even looked there. But if they won't come with me, I'd come back here with you and serve The Maker."

"What do you mean—'serve The Maker'?" asked Puddly.

"Well, like how you've helped me," he said. "You see, Needlenose and Rabid and all the rest of the outlaws, they know *about* The Maker—they just don't follow Him. If they only knew what they were missing, I'm sure they'd want to follow Him."

"But we can't make them," argued Trasher, "and I don't think they'll ever change anyhow."

"I was one of them, Trash," Waddler reminded him, "and you helped me, and I changed . . ."

"But that was different—you were caught in a trap," Trasher argued back. "You weren't really our enemy."

"Oh yes, I was," objected Waddler. "Remember, I was the one who told where your food supply was! But let's not argue. I guess if I had not been one of them, I wouldn't care so much—but I do. They're not really as bad as they seem—they just don't know any better."

"But how do you plan to get them to follow The Maker?" persisted Trasher.

"Well, I don't know exactly," he admitted. "I guess we should just help them whenever we can. One thing we could do is to spring all those traps the Upright set—that way none of them would have to die."

"But that would be too dangerous, Waddler," Trasher reasoned. "And you, more than all of us, should know better."

"That's just it," he stressed. "I don't want them to be caught like I was."

Methuselah, who had been listening to the conversation, spoke up. "Waddler, you're a mighty fine example to all of us. You see, we ain't never thought us up a *plan* to help our enemies. We jest tried to live peaceful-like with them. But you've helped us to see that's not enough. It's mighty risky, like I said, but I know The Maker will protect you and help you. And if I know The Maker, He'll lead you right to your family. Yep, we're mighty proud of you, Son."

"Thank you, Grandfather," he said quietly. "I'd like to leave as soon as I can. I feel strong enough now."

"Shall I go with you, Waddler?" offered Trasher.

"Thanks, Trash," he replied, "but I think I need to do this alone. And besides, they might need you here."

They all retired to bed with mixed feelings—sadness at the thought of Waddler leaving, but hope and excitement about his returning again with his family. Most of all, they felt a sense of awe that The Maker would want to seek and save His lost Uprights.

CHAPTER 20

A Hero

TRASHER was both sad and glad the next morning. Sad that Waddler, whom he had come to like and respect was leaving, but glad that he would soon have his yellow scarf back. How his hopes had soared when Tidy-Paw said, "We need to remove your bandage before you go, Waddler."

Carefully she and Aunt Serenity unwound the yellow scarf still covering the stump of Waddler's tail. He stood there a little self-consciously for a minute, until the others expressed their relief that it had healed beautifully.

"The Maker be praised!" exclaimed Aunt Serenity. "Good as new!"

Tidy-Paw set right to work washing the scarf in the brook and hanging it on a tree to dry. Trasher's hopes soared even higher.

It'll be so good to get my scarf back, he thought. Not that he had minded loaning it to Waddler. He was thankful that it had been the means of stopping his blood loss. But, somehow, he felt that his scarf made him braver and gave him secret power. And in another few hours he would be wearing it again.

While anticipating this great event, Trasher joined the rest of the family as they prepared food for Waddler to take on his trip. Methuselah and Seeker drew maps for Waddler and carefully planned out the safest route for him to take. Finally, all was ready for his departure.

Trasher

A quiet sadness filled the air as the family ate breakfast. No one spoke. Each one felt a loss, even though Waddler was still with them.

Furry-Ball rubbed a tear from his eye. "Waddler," he said in a very small voice, "I'll miss you. Promise to come back, won't you?"

"I'll really miss *you*, Furry-Ball," he assured him. "And, not only will I come back, but maybe I'll bring you a playmate!"

"Who?" asked Furry-Ball excitedly.

"Wait and see," answered Waddler.

And then it was time for him to go. "Oh no!" groaned Trasher as Tidy-Paw reached for his yellow scarf and filled it with food for Waddler.

"It'll be difficult to find enough food along the way and so I've packed a supply in the scarf," she told him. Trasher's heart sank as he watched his yellow scarf disappear again.

They exchanged farewells and Methuselah called after the departing Waddler, "The Maker go with you!" Waddler waved back and disappeared into the forest.

Trasher felt ashamed of his feelings. He knew that Waddler needed the scarf to carry his food, but he had so wanted to have it back. And he especially needed it for his new plan.

It had come to him yesterday when Waddler talked about springing the traps left by the Upright. *Waddler really means to do it when he comes back,* he thought. *He's so different now that he's following The Maker. He used to be weak and wishy-*

washy, but now he's a leader. Maybe it's because he has the yellow scarf. Whatever the reason, though, I can't let him do it. He's already lost his tail—what if he loses a foot, or even his life? No, I can't let him do it. I'll have to do it myself. And before he comes back. The sooner, the better. And the worst of it is that I'll have to do it without my scarf.

Trasher had a knot in his stomach the next morning for two reasons. First, he would have to accomplish a very dangerous task without his scarf. Secondly, Posie, Puddly and Furry-Ball were being sent with him to gather food. Somehow he would have to sneak away for a short period to spring the traps.

They started off, intent on finding tender shoots and buds. Trasher, however, looked only for an opportunity to carry out his mission.

"Here's some!" Posie held up her find of delicious smelling mushrooms.

"Look at this!" yelled Puddly.

"I've got some too!" said Furry-Ball, not wanting to be left out of the competition.

Trasher alone had found nothing. Beginning to feel obvious, he said offhandedly, "I think I'll go down near the brook. There's usually something to find there." Without waiting for a response, he took off. The others looked up momentarily, but then went back to work.

Trasher felt relieved to be on his own at last. But then the old worry of not having his yellow scarf crept back into his mind. Fear began to grip him so that he thought about giving up his mission entirely, and he probably would have, but for an interruption of his thoughts.

A branch snapped. The sound came from across the brook. Climbing a tree to get a better view, Trasher was shocked to see Needlenose. *Why would he be down here during*

Methuselah called after the departing Waddler, "The Maker go with you!" Waddler waved back and disappeared into the forest.

the day? he wondered. Then the answer came to him. *He's here for the bait in those traps!*

Trasher knew what he must do. Forgetting that he had no scarf, he headed straight for the nearest trap. Silently, but quickly, as if his life depended on it, he made his way toward the deadly weapon. "Please, Dear Maker," he whispered. Then using a long stick he had picked up, he poked the trap. It jumped, and its teeth slammed shut. He slipped the chain off of the stake to which it was attached and dragged the whole thing into the brook where it disappeared. Before Needlenose arrived at the trap site, Trasher was gone and working on the next one. One by one, he sprung them until only one more remained. By this time the others had begun to worry about Trasher. They had just come to the edge of the brook when they saw him bending over the trap.

"Oh no!" shouted Puddly. "He's going for the bait!"

Before they could stop him, Trasher had the trap sprung and was dragging it down to the brook where it too disappeared into the rushing water. He turned just in time to see a surprised group of raccoons facing him.

"Oh, Trasher," sighed Posie with relief, "we thought you were trying to get the bait."

"No, Posie," he answered, "I'd never do that. I was just springing the traps. I did it for Waddler—I just couldn't let him do it after all he's been through."

Furry-Ball hugged Trasher. "You're really brave. And you know what? I think your name should be 'Treasure' not Trasher!"

"Thanks, Furry," he chuckled, "although you must admit, I did 'trash' those traps!" They all laughed.

As they started home, the three youngest had hands filled with food gathered along the way. Trasher had no food, but his heart was filled to overflowing. He knew now that it wasn't his yellow scarf that gave him special power. His strength had come from within him—put there by none other than The Maker Himself.

CHAPTER 21

An
Invitation

I F YOU'VE ever been speechless when you saw a particularly lovely scene, you know exactly how Posie felt when she and Furry-Ball peeked over the wall one day. They had come near the big house in search of food, and of course, hoped they might see their little Upright. Sure enough she was there. At first it looked like there were other Uprights with her. But at second glance, they saw that they were much smaller than she. They sat on a pale pink cloth spread on the ground, and while she moved from time to time, they did not. Furry-Ball spotted the difference immediately.

"They're not real," he said. "They're just like the ones I saw when I was in the big house, remember?"

"You're right, Furry," Posie answered. "But did you ever see anything so beautiful? Look at the clothes they have on—so full of color. And that looks like food in front of them! And she's pouring something in those little shells. Do you see how she has those pretty flowers stuck in that clear stone in the middle of the cloth? I wonder why they all have those little white leaves on their laps?" Posie had so many questions about what was happening. But of one thing she *was* sure—never had she seen anything like this in all of her life.

After a while the little Upright gathered up all the things, packed them in a basket, and waved "good-bye." Posie and Furry-Ball waved back and then hurried home to tell the family. Words tumbled out as Posie described the cloth on the ground, the smooth shells with food on them, the flowers in a clear stone shell, and the little Upright pouring a delicious smelling water in some deep shells. "Oh, if only I were an Upright!" Posie said wistfully.

Furry-Ball added his comments. "And there were two little Uprights sitting on the cloth—just like the ones I saw in the big house. They didn't move at all. We watched for a long time, but they never ate the food or drank the water. They just sat there. If I had been there, I would have eaten everything—it smelled so good!"

Posie and Furry-Ball couldn't forget what they had seen. The next morning, with hope in every step, they made their way back to the wall and climbed up. But to their dismay, there was nothing to be seen. No Upright, no cloth, no little Uprights, not even a crumb of food!

"It was there *yesterday*," said Furry-Ball a little doubtfully.

"Yes, we *did* see it," replied Posie convincingly. "But we might as well go home because she's not here today. It was just too good to be true," she thought out loud.

They had reached the top of the wall and were about to climb down when Furry-Ball spotted something out of the corner of his eye. "There's a white leaf under that rock!" he shouted.

And sure enough, there it was, barely visible. Posie wasted no time grabbing it, and her little eyes scanned it for something familiar. Then she saw a word she knew. "It's the word, 'You'," she read. "It means 'us'—it's a message for *us*," she told Furry-Ball excitedly. "I can't read the rest . . . except I think it's from our little Upright. The name starts with the snake design." Anxious to translate their new message, they raced home.

Methuselah wisely encouraged them to work on the translation themselves, and only once or twice did he step in to assist them. "You're gettin' mighty good at *my* work," he complimented them.

Each of them translated several words, but Posie put them all together. " 'You are invited for tea tomorrow. Sincerely, Sarah Shepherd.' "

"What does 'Sincerely' mean?" asked Furry-Ball.

"It means, 'I really mean it,' " replied Posie.

" 'You are invited for tea tomorrow, and I really mean it,' " he repeated.

"But does she mean *us,* Grandfather? And do you think 'Sarah Shepherd' is her name? And if it does mean us, when should we go? And . . ."

Methuselah broke in at this point. "One question at a time, Little Flower. Now as to who she's a meanin' when she says 'you'—that d'pends on iffen she saw you and Furry-Ball yesterday."

"Yes, she did, Grandfather," said Posie. "She waved to us and we waved back."

"Well, my guess is that she's invitin' only you and Furry-Ball," he said gently. Puddly and Trasher looked dejected. "But 'twouldn't be safe iffen we didn't send your two brothers to watch out for you." Puddly and Trasher brightened. "Now as to these last two words, I b'lieve them to be the names of our little Upright. Jest like The Maker has more than one name, she's got two also . . . 'Sarah Shepherd.'"

Posie repeated her name. "Sarah Shepherd! At last, we know her name."

"That we do," said Methuselah, "But, as to when you're to go, I can't rightly say, Little Flower. All we knows is it's tomorrow."

"We could go early and just wait for her to come," suggested Furry-Ball. They all thought this would be a good idea.

The next day could not come soon enough for Posie and Furry-Ball. Posie had decided to wear her fur wreath in order to look her very best. As the four left, they looked for wildflowers along the way. In just a short time, they had gathered enough to make a small bouquet for Sarah, their little Upright. The sun was just breaking through the trees when they arrived at the wall.

"We'll wait up in this tree," said Trasher, "in case you need us." He and Puddly found a sunny branch and stretched out to warm themselves.

Posie and Furry-Ball sat on top of the wall, still in the shade, shivering. They waited. They waited some more. After a very long time, chilled to the bone, they climbed up alongside of Trasher and Puddly, stretched out in the sun, and fell fast asleep. They did not realize how many hours had passed before Sarah arrived.

A clinking sound awakened them, and looking down from their high branch in the tree, they saw her laying out shells on the pink cloth.

"It's time!" yelled Furry-Ball, almost falling out of the tree. "She's here!"

They scrambled down, dragging their wilted bouquet with them. Posie gave Furry-Ball some last-minute advice. "Don't do anything until you see her do it first, and watch me too."

Trying not to look too eager, they walked politely up to the pink cloth that Sarah had placed on the ground. Next to her sat the two small Uprights who had been there before. And then they saw it—a raccoon sitting absolutely still alongside. Posie and Furry-Ball froze in terror. The other raccoon did not move. After several moments of exchanged stares, Furry-Ball whispered, "He's not saying anything, and he smells funny!"

"Well, say something to him," Posie whispered back. Furry-Ball did, but there was no response.

"He's either from another country or he's really rude, 'cause he won't say anything!" Furry-Ball added. "I think he's like all those cold Uprights—I'm pretty sure he's not real, after all."

"He certainly doesn't look like one of our enemies, Furry," said Posie, "but keep an eye on him in case he moves."

Sarah sat down at one corner of the cloth, so Posie and Furry-Ball followed her example and sat down opposite her. Then, reaching across, Posie handed her wilted bouquet to Sarah.

"She likes it!" whispered Posie, when she saw Sarah's upturned mouth. And then it hit her—the realization that here they were, sitting with an Upright, about to have tea. "How wonderful to be an Upright for just a little while," she thought. She determined to do everything right—just like Sarah did.

And then it hit her—the realization that here they were, sitting with an Upright, about to have tea.

First, Sarah put her white leaf on her lap. (Of course, this was a napkin, but Posie and Furry-Ball didn't know about such things.) Posie did the same thing perfectly and signaled Furry-Ball to do so too. He followed her example, but it slid off his lap. He picked it up and tried again, but it slid off once more. Determined, the third time he held it in his paw. Sarah then reached over to help him and tied the napkin securely around his neck. After this she proceeded to tie one around the other raccoon's neck too.

"He can't do it either," Furry-Ball thought.

Then Sarah bowed her head. Posie and Furry-Ball copied her movement, but they weren't sure what this meant. As Sarah talked on and on, Furry-Ball saw something out of the corner of his eye—it was yellow and looked very tasty. He reached over carefully and placed his paw on it. He was just about to lift it to his mouth when Sarah finished talking and looked up. Furry-Ball quickly withdrew his paw, but too late. There was a paw print, right smack in the middle of the yellow food. He licked his paw, hoping to cover up the evidence that he had made the paw print, but Posie's disapproving glance told him that she had seen everything. Sarah didn't seem to notice, though.

"I wonder when we're going to eat," asked Furry-Ball, his voice a bit too loud.

"Wait, Furry, wait," whispered Posie.

Then, very gracefully, Sarah passed a plate filled with delicious smelling goodies—among them, the yellow food with Furry-Ball's paw print. Ever mindful of her manners, Posie took only one piece of each. Furry-Ball, however, took three or four of everything, in spite of Posie's glares. Thinking that perhaps it wasn't very polite to take so many pieces of food at one time, he stuffed as much into his mouth as he could, once again, to get rid of the evidence.

Posie was amazed at Sarah's ability to pour tea into the deep shells without missing. She decided right then to learn the secret and watched her carefully. Taking advantage of this moment, Furry-Ball looked around for more food. He felt it wouldn't be right to take any more from the big plate, and so when he saw that the silent raccoon next to him had a plate filled with food, and wasn't eating, he swept the food onto his own plate with one motion.

"He doesn't need it—he's not real anyway," he said to himself, trying to justify his actions.

When Posie and Sarah next looked at him, they saw a very polite little raccoon eating daintily. Sarah offered him some more sandwiches and mints. He took only a few this time, and Posie smiled approvingly. Everything seemed to be going much better until Furry-Ball remembered another polite thing to do—wash his food. He did so at once, dipping his food into the tea, which promptly overflowed onto the cloth. Sarah looked shocked. Furry-Ball realized why she seemed so surprised—she had not been washing her food. Suddenly, he had a great desire to teach this little Upright about politeness. After all, it wasn't her fault she didn't know about washing food. He demonstrated his skill once more and then looked up at her. She was watching carefully. Then she did an amazing thing. To Posie's horror, Sarah washed her own food!

"Did you see that? She caught on right away!" he whispered excitedly.

Posie was beginning to wonder if it had been a wise thing to bring Furry-Ball along. His lack of manners was a continuing embarrassment to her. Right at that moment, Sarah was pouring his *fourth* cup of tea. Posie loved it too—it had a way of warming you from your tail to your ears. But why did he have to drink so much? Perhaps it was her glare or perhaps it was his nervousness, but Furry-Ball lost control of his cup and it spilled all over the pink cloth. Sarah graciously wiped it up and tried to smile at them both.

Furry-Ball's loud burp, plus the spilled cup, and all of his poor manners put together, convinced Posie that they would never again be invited for tea. Her eyes filled with tears and her head hung down. Furry-Ball felt so ashamed when he saw Posie's reaction that he hung his head too. At any moment he expected to be asked to leave, but instead nothing happened. They sat that way for a long time, not knowing what to do.

Posie was just about to leave voluntarily, taking Furry-Ball with her, when the little Upright spoke.

Looking up, Posie saw Sarah holding something out toward Furry-Ball. It was small, but wrapped in lovely gold paper with ribbon to match, obviously a present. At first, she thought Sarah was making a mistake. She couldn't be handing it to Furry-Ball—not after what he had done. But that was exactly what she was doing, and Posie was upset (and a little bit jealous).

"You don't deserve it one bit," she whispered angrily.

"I know," he admitted. "But I just couldn't seem to help it."

Meanwhile, Methuselah had followed his grandchildren to the wall to observe from a discreet distance, this little "tea party." He chuckled to himself as he imagined what he would have done as a youngster at such a party. Probably, pretty much what Furry-Ball had done, he had to admit. And then, Sarah's eyes met his. She smiled and waved. Methuselah lifted one paw and returned the greeting! And then it was time to go. He withdrew quickly before the others realized that Sarah had waved to him.

The next thing they knew, they were waving "good-bye" and climbing over the wall. Joined by Puddly and Trasher, who were full of questions, they hurried home.

Posie still fretted over Furry-Ball's manners. "You shouldn't have eaten so much, and why did you have to spill your tea?"

"I guess I did eat a little too much," he said, "but it was so good I just couldn't stop. And I didn't mean to spill my tea—it slipped right out of my hand—it was very slippery, you see, and that soft white leaf—well it just wouldn't stay on my lap. I guess I did everything wrong, didn't I?"

Posie began to feel sorry for scolding Furry-Ball. "Well, it really wasn't all your fault, Furry. You did the best you could. After all, you haven't been to any tea parties before. And I guess Sarah didn't mind, because she *did* give the present to you."

And then they were home. The whole family gathered around Furry-Ball to watch him unwrap the package.

"You can have the gold leaf and the ribbon, Posie," he

offered. "And I don't deserve this present, so whatever it is I'll share with the whole family."

When at last the package was unwrapped, they all recognized it at once. "The Book!" they exclaimed.

"That it is," confirmed Methuselah.

CHAPTER 22

The
Book

THE BOOK! They couldn't seem to get enough of it. Methuselah's whistle woke them up earlier each day, but no one seemed to mind. They raced to get their work done, so as to get in on some of the exciting translation, and even discussed it at mealtime. It didn't take them as long as before to translate with all this practice. In fact, it had become almost like reading. As each page was read, they felt as if they were putting together a big puzzle and each piece was crucial. Some pages made them feel elated, but others made them sad. Regardless of their response, they realized what a wonderful gift it was, and The Book became their most cherished possession.

In the evenings after supper, they would often re-tell the stories they had read. Posie loved the ones about how The Maker healed Uprights. She would shut her eyes and try to imagine just how it was. "I just knew He could heal them!" she would exclaim.

Puddly seemed most intrigued with how The Maker walked on water. "It didn't work for me," he admitted after secretly trying it.

Furry-Ball told the wind to stop one day, after hearing the story of how The Maker had calmed the wind and waves, but the wind continued blowing. "He must be very strong," he said. "I wonder how He did it!"

Methuselah's remark was the most confusing of all. "He's called the Lamb of God," he told them.

"Did He become a lamb, Grandfather?" asked Posie.

"Nope—don't believe He did, Little Flower," he answered. "Most likely He was *like* a lamb in some way."

"I wish it had said He was like a raccoon instead," Posie thought out loud.

"Maybe we can be mighty thankful He's not," Methuselah answerd in a strange voice.

"Why, Grandfather?"

"Because it says the Lamb of God 'takes away the sin' of them Uprights, that's why," he continued in the same strange voice.

Posie didn't like that tone. It sounded very ominous and dreadful.

Methuselah tried to sound more cheerful. "That'll be a right wonderful day, Little Flower, when He does what He came to do."

"But how will He do it, Grandfather?" Posie could not forget the tone in Methuselah's voice.

"Can't rightly say," he answered.

Posie's thoughts went back to what her Grandfather had told her long ago—how The Maker had used the skins of animals, perhaps lambs, to clothe the Uprights in The Garden. She wondered if The Maker had to die like those innocent animals. She voiced her concern. "Does He have to *die*, Grandfather?"

"Can't rightly say," he repeated.

"It's beginning to look that way," broke in Seeker. With that, he turned ahead in The Book to a picture near the back. They stared at the picture in disbelief. There was The Maker! He was standing with His hands tied together and a wreath of thorns on His head. He wore a purple cape, but in spite of everything, he looked like a king. The expression in His eyes drew Posie's pity—they were filled with sadness. And no wonder—how could they treat Him this way? But Posie felt that this picture was not the end of the story and her dread increased.

Before they could discuss the meaning of the picture, Puddly's shout interrupted their thoughts. "It's Waddler! He's back! And he's got someone with him. Whoever he is, he's *very* small!"

They all stopped and looked up. And then they saw them coming into the clearing. Sure enough, it was Waddler, and with him, a small raccoon companion.

"I promised you I'd bring a playmate, Furry-Ball," laughed Waddler. "Meet your brother, Sunshine!"

With a stunned expression on his face, Furry-Ball exclaimed, *"My brother?"*

"Yes, I really *am* your brother, Furry-Ball," Sunshine said convincingly.

Waddler stepped forward. "I'll explain," he promised. "But first let me tell you how good it is to be home!"

They all welcomed Waddler and the new arrival.

"We thought you might not come back," admitted Puddly.

"Or that you might decide to stay," added Posie.

"I was worried that something had happened to you, Waddler," Trasher confessed.

"I always wanted a brother!" said Furry-Ball, who had not taken his eyes off the new little raccoon.

"Well, let me tell you all about him," began Waddler.

"You two look mighty hungry," said Aunt Serenity. She bustled about getting them a meal while the others gathered around Waddler and Sunshine to hear the story.

*Waddler and
Sunshine*

Waddler then told his incredible tale—how The Maker had indeed been with him and led him to his family's first home. There it was that he found what remained of them. Besides Sunshine, only his older brother and a younger sister were left. He learned that, in fleeing from the big Upright machine, they, along with Waddler's parents, had crossed the brook and later found themselves trapped by the fire. His aging parents had died in the flames, and his brother and sister thought that Furry-Ball, born on that side of the brook along with Sunshine, was also a victim. Having rescued Sunshine first, they returned to find Furry-Ball gone. They had searched for him until the fire came within inches, and then fled, expecting never to see him again. It was Waddler who had put the pieces together and realized that Furry-Ball was indeed his little brother. Seeing Sunshine confirmed this fact—he looked exactly like Furry-Ball.

Waddler shared with the family his happiness over being reunited with his brothers and sister. They had laughed over old times together, and then had gotten caught up on recent news. Waddler told them how it was that he lost his tail and all about his new family who had saved him. He shared with them all that he had learned about The Maker and how his new family tried to please The Maker by the way they lived. They had confessed their frustration, living back there with the others who didn't believe in The Maker. They told him that they had always been interested in learning more about The Maker and would like nothing more than to come and be a part of this new way. And they had so wanted to see Furry-Ball again. After much discussion they had come to a decision. Sunshine would go on ahead with Waddler while they made preparations to leave. They would await Waddler's return and then come as he guided the way.

What a celebration they shared that night! Aunt Serenity brought out some wonderful treats left them by the little Upright, and then it was their turn to tell Waddler all that had happened while he was gone.

"I sprang those traps so you wouldn't have to, Wad," Trasher explained.

"Thanks, Trash," Waddler's eyes spoke his appreciation.

"We were invited to a tea party by Sarah—that's her name, you know," said Posie with pride.

"And she gave us a gift," put in Furry-Ball. He ran to get it.

As Waddler looked at their new treasure, his eyes widened with excitement. "The Book!" he exclaimed. "And it's ours?"

"Yes, it is," and they told him all the things which they had learned.

When they were all talked out, they looked over at Furry-Ball and Sunshine. The two had fallen asleep, their arms linked together.

"It looks like they've been brothers all their lives," thought Posie.

$\mathcal{E}$The xchange

"CATCH me!" yelled Furry-Ball to his new little brother early the next morning. Posie smiled as she watched the two. A brother almost his own age was just what Furry-Ball needed. And yet she wondered if he would forget her, now that Sunshine had come.

Furry-Ball answered her silent question. Taking a break from his chasing, he came over to her and sat down. "Posie," he said in a thoughtful tone of voice, "will you still be my sister?"

"Yes, Furry," she answered. "You see, you don't have to have just one family—you can have two! And I can be your 'heart sister.'"

"Will you be *more* my sister or *less?*" he probed.

"I think *more*, Furry," she assured him.

"Good!" he said and ran off to play with Sunshine again.

The next days were filled with joy as the family and Sunshine got better acquainted. He was a delight to them all, always ready to play at a moment's notice and almost always cheerful. But there were times when Furry-Ball and Sunshine argued too. More than once it was Puddly who took on the task of teaching them how to share and be a team.

"The Book says to be kind, one to another," he constantly reminded them.

One rainy day, when the older members of the family were deeply engrossed in translating The Book, Furry-Ball and Sunshine almost came to blows. "It's mine!" yelled Furry-Ball.

"Is not! It's mine!" Sunshine answered back. They were fighting over a dried leaf that had blown in the doorway.

The rest of the family exchanged annoyed glances.

"Hush, children," said Aunt Serenity, who seldom got irritated.

This unusual reaction from Aunt Serenity was not lost on Puddly. "Trash, can I talk to you a minute—it's important," he signaled. The two found a quiet corner and Puddly began.

"We're not getting an awful lot done these days with those two always fighting right under our noses. I think if they had some toys of their own, they'd fight less."

"You're right, Puddly, but we don't have any toys for them."

"Well, I could give them my ball. I don't really need it anymore—now that we have The Book. I find it much more interesting reading The Book than just playing with an old ball, anyway."

"Well, the problem with that is that they'd just fight over the ball. Unless, of course, I give one of them my yellow scarf," added Trasher in a quiet voice.

"Oh no, Trash! Not your scarf! I didn't mean for you to give up your scarf!" Puddly's reaction was one of alarm.

"Why not? You're giving up your ball," he said with no regret. "Besides, you're right, The Book is much more interesting—and I don't need my scarf anymore." The two came back to the family circle and presented Furry-Ball and Sunshine with their new gifts.

"For us?" they asked incredulously.

"Yes, but no more fighting!" Puddly used his sternest voice.

"We won't ever fight again!" promised Furry-Ball.

All the others smiled at this remark, and then turned back in relief to their translation efforts. All except Posie. She had watched this whole scene with interest and a little bit of envy. With interest because she never thought she'd see the day when her two brothers would part with their dearest treasures, and with envy because she herself had nothing to give her little brothers, and she saw how happy they were to receive the gifts. Her dearest treasure was her fur wreath that she wore only on special occasions. But Furry-Ball and Sunshine would not be interested in this, she was sure. If only she had something she could give them! And then the thought came to her, *Why not look for something?* Surely if she searched carefully she could find something of value. She looked outside and noticed the rain had stopped. "I'm going out to look for flowers for my wreath," she announced. (*And for a gift for the boys,* she said to herself.)

She was excited as she ventured forth on her search. Her fur wreath made her feel that this was a special mission and she could hardly wait 'til she found the gift. Whatever it was, she was sure she'd recognize it. She scurried along quickly, but her eyes missed nothing. Once she saw a bright sparkle of color. Upon closer investigation, she discovered it to be clear green stone, but the edges were sharp and jagged.

Too dangerous for them, she thought and walked on. Pine cones covered the path, but that would not be special enough for her brothers, she knew, and she walked further.

After a very long time, she became discouraged and stopped to rest. Looking around her, she realized she was almost in sight of the wall. *Why not climb up and see if Sarah is there?* she thought. *After all, Grandfather approves of her.* She climbed up swiftly and peeked over. Sarah was there all right, but so were other Uprights hurrying in and out of the big house.

At one point, all the Uprights went in, but they did not shut the door. Posie was curious. She had never seen the inside of the big house that Furry-Ball had described—the part that went "up." Jumping down from the wall, she crept nearer until she reached a small bush right near the steps. Her curiosity was momentarily dampened when a stream of Uprights came out again and then, a little later, entered once more.

Maybe I really shouldn't be here, she thought. But as the noise of the Uprights stopped, she felt much safer. She waited. Nothing happened. She waited some more. Still nothing happened. Finally, her nose twitched with curiosity and she carefully edged herself toward the open door-way.

"If an Upright comes, I won't do what Furry did—I'll run away," she instructed herself. Peeking around the door, her eyes scanned the room. She saw stairs. *Just what Furry described,* she said to herself. Cautiously, she crept up the stairs, ready to run at the slightest noise. There was none, and so she climbed to the top. There before her was a long red path, lined on either side by long rows of chairs. But at the end of the red path was a high table covered with a beautiful purple cloth. Something drew her down that red path to an object on the table. Not an Upright was in sight, so she crept nearer to see what it was. Then she recognized it and shrank back in terror—a wreath of thorns. She re-

called the picture of The Maker wearing it—it looked exactly like the one in the picture.

Many thoughts went through Posie's mind in that instant, some very confusing. *Has He worn it already? Or do they plan on using it soon?* She heard voices. Anger and despair welled up in Posie's heart. She could not take a chance, in an instant her decision was made. If they planned on using this terrible thing on The Maker, she was going to stop it. She ran up to the table, grabbed the purple cloth and pulled herself up. There it was facing her, and never had she seen an object that frightened her more. Seizing the wreath of thorns, she was just about to run away with it, when she remembered something. She did not have the right to take something that was not hers—not even this terrible thing.

"All right," she said angrily, "I'll give them *my* wreath instead. That's what He should wear anyway, not this!" She looked at the ugly wreath with its treacherous sharp thorns. She remembered those sad eyes in the picture. Then tenderly and lovingly she removed her fur wreath and laid it down in place of the wreath of thorns. "It's for you, Dear Maker."

Seizing the thorn wreath she ran from the building, all the way to the edge of the brook, the sharp thorns of the wreath biting into her as she ran. There, panting and sobbing, she threw the hateful thing in and watched it as the rushing water carried it out of sight. And then she cried some more, feeling her very heart would break. "Why would those Uprights want to hurt their Maker?" she questioned out loud.

After a long time, feeling somewhat better, she got up and slowly made her way home. When at last she entered the clearing, no one asked her why she didn't have a wreath. They could tell she was greatly upset and knew she would tell them about it in her own time. Posie felt sad that she still had no gift for the boys. But as she fell asleep that night, she thought of the gift she had given The Maker, and she was glad.

CHAPTER 24

The Sickness

R ABID is sick!" Trasher's startling announcement got everyone's attention.

"Are you sure, Trash?" questioned Puddly.

"I saw him myself," he replied. "He's trying to get to the brook. I hope the others come and help him. But if they don't, I'm afraid he won't make it—he looks very weak."

"No, they won't, Trash," said Waddler flatly. "They're afraid of sickness. They'll just leave him to die."

"But they can't do that, Wad," protested Puddly. "That's just plain murder."

No one spoke for a minute or two as the hopelessness of Rabid's condition hit them. Then Seeker decided that they needed to assess the situation again, and suggested that Trasher, Puddly, Waddler and he go back to the brook to see what could be done. When they got there they realized it was all true. Rabid lay piteously in a heap near the water, seemingly unable to go any further. He groaned now and then.

"I know you *all* want to help him," said Seeker, "but we need to talk about who should go. Sickness can mean death," he warned. They returned home, deeply troubled and apprehensive about the decision that lay before them.

Since Waddler had shared his concern for their enemies, they had all come to see this as a mission. But other than Trasher's springing of the traps, they had not yet had an opportunity to help their enemies. Now came the chance and they all saw it.

"I think I should go," stated Waddler. "Rabid knows me best."

"Your family is depending on you to come back, Wad," argued Trasher. "I should go. Besides, you've been through so much already."

"I'll go," offered Puddly. "He knows me too—I've talked to him before."

"It's too risky for you children," interrupted Seeker. "It's settled—I'm going."

"Not quite," added Methuselah. "It's me who's a-goin'!" All eyes turned toward him.

"Not *you*, Grandfather!" gasped Puddly. "You can't go!"

"That I can, Son," he repeated. "I'm the one who should go."

"But why you, Grandfather?" Puddly pressed.

"'Cause I'm the oldest, and if something were to happen, it might as well happen to me," he said with authority.

Posie shuddered at his words. It was bad enough to think of the possibility of something happening to The Maker, and now Methuselah. A tear trickled down her cheek.

"Let me go, please, Grandfather," she begged. "I don't want anything to happen to you. What if you were to die?"

"Now, now, Little Flower, it's not for certain that I'll die—it's jest a risk. And I'm the one most prepared to take that risk. And with The Maker a-healin' all them Uprights, jest maybe The Maker'll provide, iffen I should get the sickness."

A ray of hope filled Posie. Maybe The Maker could heal her grandfather if he got the sickness as He had healed all those Uprights in the stories from The Book. She felt better, and quietly decided to ask The Maker for His help.

Plans were made by the whole family as to how to best help Rabid. It was decided that Methuselah should take a shell filled with water and try to get Rabid to drink. They were sure that this was his greatest need. They all accompanied Methuselah to the edge of the brook, but only he crossed over. Slowly, he approached Rabid.

"I've come to help you, Son," said Methuselah quietly. Rabid did not move. Methuselah bent over the weakened form of his enemy. He put the shell to his mouth, and drop by drop, poured the life-giving liquid down his parched throat. Rabid's eyes opened slightly, then closed. With great effort, he spoke one word.

"Why?" was all that he could ask.

"The Maker's orders, Son," responded Methuselah. He placed some soft straw under his head.

"Thank you," whispered Rabid. Then he was quiet.

Methuselah walked to the edge of the brook. "I'll not be a-comin' home today," he told the others across the water. "I've touched the sickness," he explained, "and b'sides, he can't take too much water at one time. He'll be a-needin' more shortly I 'xpect. You all go on home."

Methuselah turned away and lay down near Rabid to watch and wait. Eyes filled with tears, the others left their side of the brook and made their way home to wait also.

During the long night, Methuselah was awakened by familiar cackles and taunts. "You got the sickness, yet, Pops? Won't take but a day or two more and you'll be just like him," they jeered. "No fool like an old fool," they yelled as they left.

Over and over, Methuselah got up, filled the shell and gently poured drops of water onto Rabid's swollen tongue. By morning, he himself was thirsty and famished. Heading down to the brook, he was surprised to find his family already there with a delicious meal prepared by Tidy-Paw and Aunt Serenity. They laid the food carefully on a rock in the middle of the water and then returned to the other side. Methuselah waded out and took the much-needed food to the opposite shore. After he was refreshed, he and the others exchanged news across the water. Then he returned and attempted to feed Rabid some of the solid food he had saved out. Completing this task, he called across the brook once more to give them the news.

"When can you come back, Grandfather?" yelled Posie.

"Iffen I don't have the sickness by tomorrow, Little One, and Rabid gets his strength back, I'll be a-comin' home for supper," he answered.

Posie shuddered, as she thought, *But what if you don't come home for supper?*

The day went slowly for all of them as they waited to see what would happen. Methuselah continued to give Rabid more water and a small amount of food. Little by little, Rabid's strength returned. He could talk a little, and he and Methuselah chatted from time to time. But as the evening approached, Methuselah grew more and more tired and napped frequently between Rabid's feeding.

In the morning, the family once again gathered at their side of the brook. But this time, Methuselah was not there. Their worst fears were realized—he had the sickness.

CHAPTER 25

The Cure

POSIE was frantic with fear. And yet, oddly enough, she felt an inner calmness come over her. She remembered Methuselah's words, spoken the day before. In case he got the sickness, she had planned out just what she would do. She rushed home to carry out her plan. Carefully she wrote the same message that she had written before on a white leaf they had saved—"H.E.L.P." But this time she added three more words—words that she had painstakingly translated from the Code—"Methuselah is sick." Then, running as fast as she could, she headed for the big house hoping to find the little Upright she now knew as Sarah.

She climbed over the wall and sighed with relief to see her sitting by the tall stone. Then, waiting until the little Upright saw her, she placed the letter on the ground and backed a short distance away. Sarah came over and read the letter, and tucking it into her pocket, she ran into the big house. After what seemed like a very long time, the little Upright returned with something in her hand and reached out toward Posie. The same feeling of trust as before filled her and she crept forward to take the object. It was wrapped in a white leaf as soft as fur. Posie took it, waved her other paw and ran back with it to the brook.

When at last she stopped running, Posie unwrapped the tiny package and saw only a very small object—white, disc-shaped, and hard, like a rock. At first, she thought it was sweet "rock food." She scratched off a small amount of the substance and licked her paw. The taste was bitter. *Is this all?* Disappointment filled her. But, overcoming her discouragement, she reminded herself that once before when she had asked The Maker, He had sent help through the little Upright. Maybe it was so now, even though the tiny white object didn't look very promising and didn't taste very good either.

As she neared the edge of the brook, she saw the others still waiting.

"He doesn't answer us," reported Puddly. "He just lies there."

Posie didn't have time for conversation. Before they could stop her, she picked up a shell and, filling it with water, began to wade across the brook.

"Come back!" shouted Seeker.

"I won't touch him, Father, I'll be careful," she promised. "He needs water and . . . something else."

The others stood motionless in horrified silence as Posie brought the shell of water within reach of Methuselah.

"Grandfather," she begged, "take this water, please, Grandfather, please." She waited. Methuselah's paw reached out slowly. Grasping the shell, very gradually he brought it to his mouth. Then came her moment. Posie dropped the white disc-shaped rock into the water, just as Methuselah drank it. She watched, expecting to see her grandfather healed immediately. When nothing happened, Posie turned away sadly. Her grandfather was still sick. As she reached the edge of the brook, Rabid called out to her.

"Water," he said, "I need water."

Posie picked up another shell at the brook's edge and filled it. She brought it within his reach and then stood back. He seized it and drank thirstily. As she brought water in another shell, she glanced over at Methuselah once more. His eyes opened and he spoke.

"Thank you, Little Flower, thank you." Posie hurried to fill his shell a second time. Bending over him, she longed to be able to touch him. Right then, it didn't seem to matter to her even if she got the sickness. Just as she reached out to stroke his fur, Seeker yelled from across the water.

"No, Posie, no!"

She withdrew her hand, but as she did so, she realized she had never before felt quite so alone. She crossed the brook in obedience to her father. In quiet tones, she told the others what she had done—how she had asked The Maker to heal Methuselah, and how she had written a message to Sarah for help. Then she confessed her disappointment in The Maker when the tiny rock didn't make Methuselah better.

"But Grandfather spoke to you, Posie," said Trasher encouragingly. "He wasn't able to speak before he drank the water with the little rock. Maybe it's working."

They decided to stay at the brook all night. Every hour or so, Posie crossed over and poured more water in the shells of the two sick raccoons, always being careful not to touch them.

As morning dawned, a whistle broke the silence. Posie looked up. There was Methuselah standing on the other side, as if he were completely well again.

"Ain't someone goin' to bring me some breakfast?" he complained. Then he whistled some more, this time waking them all up. They stared in disbelief.

"Grandfather," exclaimed Posie, "He *did* heal you, He *did!*"

"Calm down, Little Flower," laughed Methuselah. "That He did—at least I'm on the mend. And 'twould be a right nice gesture iffen you'd bring me some food," he hinted again rather strongly.

They all ran for his food at once, and brought the rest of the family back with them to see for themselves.

Methuselah continued to gain strength rapidly that day, though Rabid's progress was slower. Posie refused to leave the other side of the brook except for one time, and only then in order to bring The Book. She was quite certain he would not die from the sickness now, and wanting to keep him company, she was sure The Book would help. Translating took much longer for her than for her Grandfather, but the stories kept their minds off the sickness and on The Maker and this seemed to help.

Posie read some of their favorite stories of how The Maker had healed Uprights and interspersed her reading with many questions. But the question that burned most deeply in her mind was "How could The Maker heal their hearts?" Once, when Methuselah dozed off, she thought to herself, *I'll just read ahead a little, and maybe I can find out. Then when Grandfather wakes up, I'll go back to where we left off.* She turned to the picture of The Maker wearing the wreath of sharp thorns. She *had* to know what happened. "I'll go back and find out why those Uprights did this to Him," she decided.

But the moment she did this, she was sorry she had. When she read how The Maker was arrested and spat on and beaten, she found herself protesting with thoughts like, *This can't be true!* and *Why do they hate Him so?* and *If only they knew who He was! Surely He'll tell them!*

By the time Methuselah awoke, Posie was in tears.

He was quick to notice and asked, "Somethin' troublin' you, Little Flower?"

"Oh, Grandfather, it's terrible! It says in The Book that they hate Him. And not only that, they arrested Him for no reason, and beat Him, and it's true—they *did* put a wreath of sharp thorns on His head. I knew it—I just knew it was true!" she began to sob.

"Now, now, Little Flower, iffen I know The Maker, He'll make some good come of it. Read on," he encouraged her.

Posie did, but the story seemed to get worse. Methuselah tried to stop her, but she had already read too far. "Oh, they can't do this to Him—they can't!" she cried, her heart nearly breaking. But it was altogether true—she had just read it in The Book. They had killed The Maker. They'd hung Him by nails on a wooden cross. He was dead.

Posie buried her head in Methuselah's fur and sobbed for a long time. Methuselah's heart was heavy too but he wanted to spare Posie's tender feelings. "Time you was a-gettin' back home to bed, Little Flower. Iffen I know The Maker, it's not the end."

Posie obeyed, but she promised to return in the morning with food and The Book. How she hoped Methuselah was right—if only this weren't the end.

Morning came too quickly for Posie. She didn't mind taking food to her grandfather, but how she dreaded reading the rest of the story. Weighed down with gloomy thoughts, she was not prepared to see her grandfather already up and busily scooping up water at the brook.

"Mornin', Little Flower!" It was as if Methuselah had forgotten that The Maker was dead.

Together, they brought food and water to Rabid, and then sat apart and shared their own breakfast. Posie felt a little cheered by this, in spite of herself.

Methuselah opened The Book and began reading to himself.

"Yep. I thought so!" he confirmed with a smile on his face.

Posie's nose twitched with curiosity. "What, Grandfather, what?"

"Didn't stay dead, that's what! The Maker's alive, Little Flower, alive!" Methuselah threw back his head and laughed—a laugh of joy, of relief and a laugh of victory! Even Posie joined in and together they laughed until big tears rolled down their cheeks.

When at last she stopped, Posie said, "I'm so glad,

Grandfather. I'm *so* glad! The Maker's even stronger than Death then, isn't He?"

"That He is, Child, that He is!"

"Grandfather, if The Maker's stronger than Death, why did He let them kill Him in the first place? He could have stopped them."

"Yep, that's a fact," he agreed. "But maybe He chose to die."

"Chose to die?" she repeated. "But why?"

"So's them Uprights wouldn't have to die for their own wrongdoin'."

Posie was stunned. "He died for *them?*" she asked. "Because of what *they* did?"

"'Pears so, Little Flower."

"He must have really loved them!" she concluded.

"Yep, it must have been The Maker's punishment for wrong—Death—and He took it Himself—the only way He could heal their hearts."

Methuselah and Posie headed for home that night, since he was well again and it was safe to return to the others. They would come back to help Rabid in the morning. Posie slept soundly for the first time in many nights.

CHAPTER 26

The Sacrifice

RAIN was falling softly outside the next morning as Posie opened her eyes. She rubbed the sleep out to see more clearly, but the skies were so gray and the forest so filled with mist that her sight was not much better. Quietly, she made her way down to breakfast, and was surprised to find Methuselah already up. He was sitting under a low-hanging evergreen branch reading The Book.

In spite of the dreary day, Posie greeted him cheerfully. "Good morning, Grandfather!"

"Mornin', Little Flower. This here's mighty interestin'!"

"What, Grandfather? Have you learned something new?"

"That I have, and it's not s'prisin'!"

Posie sighed. If only it didn't take him so long to tell things. But she waited patiently until he continued.

"Seems as if The Maker can make dead Uprights alive . . . once they take the gift."

"The gift?" A puzzled expression came across her face.

"Yep. When they take the gift He gives 'em. Y'see, He gave His life in trade for theirs. To put it plain and simple, He died so they don't have to die. And iffen they jest reach out and take the gift, He'll make them alive."

"But how do they take the gift, and do you mean they won't die at all?" asked Posie.

"Well, y'see, Little Flower, them Uprights may not have masks on their faces, but they have 'em in their hearts. They've got to be willin' to take off those masks and open their hearts to The Maker. It's with their hearts they reach out and take the gift, The Book says. And since The Maker Himself went through death, t'wouldn't be fair iffen they didn't too, but The Book says they won't stay dead. He'll make them alive forever, jest like He is—iffen they take the gift."

"How wonderful! What good news, Grandfather! And you're right, it's *not* surprising!" she agreed. "But Grandfather, what about us?"

"Well, Little Flower, in all my readin' and studyin' so far, I haven't come across any word on us raccoons. 'Course, I did find the words Uncle Seth used to say about the sparrows—that The Maker doesn't forget a one of them. And seein' there's more of them than of us, I think it's right safe for us to b'lieve that He won't forget one of us, neither. But, we'll keep a-readin' and studyin' in case there's a word about us folks."

The rain continued to fall, a steady dripping rain. Tidy-Paw and Aunt Serenity were already up preparing the meal at their "rainy-day" table under a nearby bough when, one by one, the others awoke and straggled in.

"I think Rabid will eat more today," suggested Posie as she watched Aunt Serenity pack a food bundle for their sick enemy.

"The Maker be praised!" exclaimed Aunt Serenity. "That he will!" She added some freshly picked wild strawberries. "Furry-Ball and Sunshine will be here soon with the rest of our food if they ever remember what it is they were sent to do," she chuckled. "But like as not, they're playin' 'chase me' instead," she said and chuckled again.

No sooner had she said these words than into the clearing rushed Furry-Ball and Sunshine. "Did you hear it?" they shouted. "Did you hear it?"

"Calm down, Boys, calm down," urged Aunt Serenity. "Catch your breath and tell us what you heard."

"It was awful," burst out Furry-Ball.

"We heard lots of running, so we hid," added Sunshine. "And then they came!"

"Who?" demanded Tidy-Paw.

"The bandits—Needlenose and the rest of them," answered Furry-Ball. "They were laughing because they had just raided an Upright's chicken coop."

"And the Upright was running after them—with a death stick! And then came the noise—and it was awful!" Sunshine began to sob.

"There, there, Sunshine," Aunt Serenity said softly as she stroked his fur.

"Needlenose and his gang got away, but the Upright is still coming—and he's coming toward the brook!" exclaimed Furry-Ball.

Methuselah had walked into the circle at this point followed by the others, and all eyes turned toward him.

"The one who's most in danger is Rabid—he's lyin' there helpless unless we protect him. Posie, Puddly and I will go to the brook to help him. But Trasher, you go with your father to see about headin' off the Upright. The rest of you stay here and hide—and may The Maker go with us."

Methuselah and the two children were at the brook in no time, but they found Rabid still asleep. Angry dark clouds filled the sky. The dripping rain had now become a downpour. The three raccoons huddled together for a moment as Methuselah gave instructions.

"You help Puddly prepare a bed under that bough, Little Flower." He unpacked the food bundle and gently tried to wake Rabid.

Meanwhile, Seeker and Trasher raced through the forest until they heard the running footsteps of the Upright. It was true—he was coming nearer and nearer to the brook. In fact, he was only minutes away from Rabid.

"Let's try to distract him, Trasher, but don't get out in the open," warned Seeker. Remembering Puddly's trick, he said, "If it worked for Puddly, maybe it'll work for us."

They hurried on, thickets and sharp branches pulling great tufts of fur off their backs as they ran, coming as near to the Upright as they dared without being seen.

"Now!" whispered Seeker. With that, Trasher rolled a big rock down a steep slope behind the Upright. Just as they expected, he wheeled around, pointed his terrible death stick and shot in that direction. Seeker and Trasher, well-hidden under a bush, froze in their tracks. The deafening explosion shattered the forest stillness. Never had they heard anything like it before. Then the Upright, not hearing any further noise, plunged on toward the brook.

"It's not going to work, Trasher," whispered Seeker, when at last they had regained their composure. "Let's hurry and get there before he does and warn Grandfather." Noiselessly they ran, swiftly covering the distance, knowing the real danger that awaited their loved ones.

By now, the rain came down in sheets, making it hard to run without slipping. But it was the darkness of the sky that foretold the dreadful events which followed. And then, everything seemed to happen at once. Yet later when they talked about it, they realized they had seen it all.

Seeker and Trasher arrived just ahead of the Upright and yelled desperately to Methuselah, "Run for your life!"

Methuselah, bending over Rabid, tried to move him to safety, but the distance was too great. Seeing his plight, Seeker and Trasher dashed into the clearing to help. Nearer and nearer came the heavy footsteps until they all knew it would be only seconds before he reached them. Posie and Puddly watched in horror from their place under the bough. And then Methuselah did an amazing thing. In a quiet, but commanding voice, he looked at Seeker and Trasher who were still helping him move Rabid, and said, "Go back!"

They obeyed instantly. Perhaps it was because they had been able to move Rabid quite near the forest edge and felt he would not easily be seen, or perhaps out of their own survival instinct they hid, but when they were able to look, none of them were prepared for what they saw.

169

Methuselah did not run. Instead, without a thought for his own safety, he stooped over Rabid, completely covering him with his own body. When he was satisfied that Rabid's body was not visible, he looked up and calmly awaited his adversary.

It seemed to Posie that the next seconds took a hundred years. A great cracking and snapping of branches told her the Upright was almost there. She held her breath. Perhaps he would miss the clearing entirely if only they could remain quiet enough. To her horror, he plunged into the opening, whirling in every direction as he sought his victim, until his eyes fixed upon Methuselah.

Posie could never forget that Upright. He was large, with a beard almost like fur and eyes as cold as ice. He seemed a little shaken when Methuselah didn't move, but only for a few seconds. Posie expected to see an angry expression on his face, but there was none. Neither was there a happy upturned mouth. That was what she remembered about him the most—no expression at all. It was as if Methuselah didn't matter to him, dead or alive. He pointed his death stick at him.

As Posie watched, tears welled up in her eyes, partially blocking out the terribleness of this moment. She couldn't move. Yet with all her strength, she tried to will her grandfather to safety. It was no use—he stayed there motionless. Somehow, in the deepest place of her heart, she knew that her grandfather was choosing to give his life for Rabid, and that she could not stop him. She wept, and even the trees seemed to weep with her, their soggy branches bending under the driving rain.

As for Methuselah, he faced the Upright without fear. In fact, there seemed to be no regret in those great eyes as he looked steadfastly at him. Posie would never forget the courage and tenderness on his magnificent face before the

*Somehow, in the deepest place of her heart, she knew
that her grandfather was choosing to give his life for Rabid,
and that she could not stop him.*

shot was fired. And then it came, shattering the forest stillness once more. Tears so filled Posie's eyes by now that she did not see it happen. Only when the Upright, with no emotion at all, turned and walked out of the clearing, did she know for sure it was over.

And then the numbness left and feeling returned. Not caring for her own safety, Posie ran to her grandfather's side and buried her face in his beautiful gray fur. "Oh Grandfather," she cried, "Oh Grandfather!" And then she wept with great heaving sobs for a very long time.

One by one, the others quietly joined Posie at Methuselah's side. No one had words, and even Posie's sobs gradually subsided. There was only silence. Methuselah's life was finished.

It was the rain that brought them to their senses as it penetrated their fur. They huddled together for warmth and began to comfort one another with words like, "How great a heart Grandfather had" and "How much he loved his enemy."

At this remembrance, Seeker gently moved Methuselah's body aside to uncover Rabid. His eyes opened slowly. In a weak and choking voice he said, "He died for *me*."

$\mathscr{H}$ope

POSIE was alone with Methuselah. She had stayed behind, not willing to leave him, even though she knew he was dead. With one paw gently laid on his, she cried herself to sleep. Even the cold rain and cutting wind did not wake her. She was totally exhausted.

Voices finally caused her to open her eyes. She was cold and wet, but relieved to see the familiar faces of her family bent over her and Methuselah's still body. There was more crying, and yet it was a comfort for Posie to cry with those who loved him as she did.

Upright footsteps interrupted their grieving and they scurried to safety under a nearby bush.

"Maybe he's come back to see if Grandfather's really dead," whispered Puddly.

"Or to shoot us too," suggested Trasher.

To their surprise, it was not the same Upright who entered the clearing—it was their little friend Sarah.

Posie strained every muscle in her body as she leaned forward to see what Sarah would do. As the little Upright ran into the clearing, she stopped and stared unbelievingly as she saw the body of Methuselah. Then, running over to his side, she fell on her knees, and covering her face with her hands, she sobbed, just as Posie herself had done.

As Posie and the others watched the little Upright, tears flowed down their own cheeks as well.

"She loved him too," concluded Furry-Ball.

And then to their amazement, Sarah took off her sweater, gently placed Methuselah's body on it and carefully lifted him in her arms. Posie saw a tear fall on Methuselah's beautiful gray fur as she carried him away from the clearing.

"I wonder where she's taking him!" they all said at once. "Let's follow quietly," urged Seeker.

They did. It was toward the big house that Sarah went. As they drew near, they found some tall trees and climbed up for a better view. They looked down just in time to see Sarah digging a deep hole near the stone wall they had so often climbed. Methuselah's body lay limp as if he were sleeping. Lining the hole with a soft grass cushion, she gently laid him to rest, covering his body with a blanket of leaves and then the final layer of soil on top. After that, she stood up, bowed her head and closed her eyes. Then, opening them, she waved her hand and before more tears fell, she turned and walked away.

"Let's go home now," suggested Seeker. They began to climb quietly down the tree. All except Posie.

"I think I'll stay and watch for a little longer," she said softly.

"Don't stay too long, Dear," cautioned Aunt Serenity.

They were gone and Posie was alone. This time there were no tears—only thoughts flooded her mind. "Why did he have to die?" she wondered out loud. "Oh, I saw what he did, I know he chose to die, but I'm so sorry that he's gone. Grandfather gave a gift to Rabid—but will he ever realize?"

*Then, running to his side, she fell on her knees, and covering
her face with her hands, she sobbed, just as Posie
herself had done.*

At this point, her thoughts were interrupted by Sarah's return. This time the little Upright knelt down and placed a small rock on the ground by Methuselah's grave. Then as quickly as she had come, she was gone. Posie jumped down to examine the rock more closely. It had writing on it, and she found to her amazement that she could translate clearly. "Here lies Methuselah," she read slowly. "He was a good and Upright raccoon."

Hope filled Posie's heart. So the little Upright thought that Methuselah was Upright. Did this mean that Methuselah would live again just as Uprights who believed in The Maker? Posie smiled. Maybe he would, or maybe he wouldn't, but all of a sudden she knew it didn't matter— she could leave it in The Maker's hands. Then she smiled again . . . a smile of discovery! *I guess he gave me a gift too,* she thought. *He gave me the gift of believing in The Maker just as he did.* She turned to leave with a new song in her heart. "There's lots to do when you serve The Maker," she reminded herself.

As she jumped down from the wall to find her way home, a dark figure stepped toward her out of the shadows. It was Rabid. "I want to follow The Maker," he announced. Posie's work had begun.

An excerpt from *Methuselah's Legacy,* coming in Fall 1995:

Furry-Ball said what they were all feeling one day. "Why don't we go see if Sarah left any apples for us on the stone wall?" he suggested. "I'm *awfully* hungry!"

"It would do us all good to have a nice meal," Seeker encouraged them. "Leave it to Furry to think of food," he chuckled. "But now that you mention it, I'm hungry too!" With that, he sent the children off to look for the apples.

Before they knew it, they were at the stone wall. And just as Furry-Ball had predicted, there were the apples. Sarah had placed them in a neat row on top of the wall.

"A letter!" shouted Puddly, the first to see it. Quickly setting the apples down, the others gathered around Puddly as he attempted to read it. "I am . . ."

"Sorry!" interjected Posie, pushing her face as close as she could to the letter.

"Methuselah . . ." continued Puddly.

"Died!" added Trasher.

Putting the words together, Puddly read, "I am sorry Methuselah died." Then translating the next sentence they were able to read, "I loved him too. Your Friend, Sarah S."

Tears filled their eyes and they became very quiet. Posie heaved a deep sigh. "We're not the only ones who are sad. Just think of how sad Sarah must feel! I saw her cry when she found Grandfather. And yet even though she feels sad, she thought of us."

"These apples are proof of that," admitted Trasher.

"And so is this letter," added Puddly. Suddenly he felt very ashamed. "We've been thinking only about ourselves."

"If only we could think of a way to cheer *her* up," sighed Posie. She began to fold the letter.

"Wait!" Sunshine was looking at the bottom of the letter. "There's more! What does this mean?"